Metanoia

Adam's Advent

RUEBEN LEFLOYD

Copyright © 2021 Rueben Lefloyd
All rights reserved
First Edition

PAGE PUBLISHING, INC.
Conneaut Lake, PA

First originally published by Page Publishing 2021

ISBN 978-1-6624-2781-7 (pbk)
ISBN 978-1-6624-2782-4 (digital)

Printed in the United States of America

To Gus, who believes I'm an eagle and not a parrot.

To Marlene, who gave the monster life.

Prologue

The wind flowed through the trees in a high-pitched whisper, carrying melodies across the landscape. Joseph saw Adam in the valley walking behind a mule; his hands wrapped in the twine across the animal's back, steering him along. He heard voices; haunting as they drifted along the edges of his dreams. Songs he didn't know but that were somehow familiar. The heat rose from the ground and enveloped his entire body; sweat rolled down his back and pooled on his lip. Adam wiped his face on his sleeve and felt the grit sting his eyes. In the background, Joseph heard shouting.

Joseph
Lugazi, Uganda

"Wake up!!"
Joseph felt the bed shake.
"Get your brother and sister!"
Joseph's mind was cloudy as he tried to comprehend what his father was saying.
"*Mwana* [son]. Wake up! Do you hear me?"
"Yes, Father."
Suddenly awake, Joseph could hear a loud commotion outside. He felt his father push a large bag onto his back. He shifted to distribute the weight while his father moved quickly around the room. Joseph's mother pushed shoes on his sister and brother's feet. Every now and then, she ran her hand across her belly, Joseph assumed to sooth her unborn daughter's fears.
"Head to the village on the other side of the river."

"Aren't you coming, Father?"

"No. Mother cannot travel. We will join you in a few days. Go! There's no time to discuss."

Joseph moved towards his four-year-old sister, Iyana, and three-year-old brother, Thomas. He took their tiny hands and moved them towards the dark hole that led to the other side of the village. Iyana was crying. Joseph turned to quiet her.

"*Nyamaza* [hush], Sister! *Kaka* [brother] is here. No one will harm you."

Joseph squeezed Izzy in a hug before pulling her towards the dark space. He handed the lantern to his younger brother and began the decent into darkness. He did not look back. The shouting from his kinsman drowned out his mother's sobs as his father pushed the rug in place and repositioned the bunk bed on top.

Joseph reached back and took the lantern from Thomas. He could still hear chaos aboveground as the neighboring tribesmen corralled the youth and boys of his village. As he moved through the darkened earth, he realized his father had never planned to use the tunnel. It was too small to accommodate his parents. Father had dug the tunnel specifically for the children in anticipation of an event of this magnitude. The thought angered Joseph as he attempted to push the fear aside that he may never see his parents again.

He stopped for a moment to determine which tunnel to follow. His father had created a detour in the event they were tracked. He'd shown Joseph what to look for to ensure he was going in the right direction: the roots of the acacia tree stood out visibly against the dark earth.

Joseph and his siblings moved quickly. The commotion from the village seemed distant, but they could hear echoes reverberating against their ear drums. As they rounded a corner, Joseph smelled the pungent odor of burning leaves. When they exited the earth, orange flames warmed their faces.

The children watched fire consume the brush as the houses in the distance crackled in the wind. The light made Joseph squint as he looked among the massive flames for anyone or anything familiar. He heard a coyote yelp in the distance. Instinctively, he pushed Iyana and Thomas into a patch of tall grass. Squatting next to them, he looked out over the valley.

In the distance, there was a tall figure walking along the edge of the brush, beating the weeds with a spear. Joseph heard someone shriek. He watched as the man dragged a woman from the brush and ran her through with a machete. Joseph stopped breathing, afraid the sound would alert the hunter to his whereabouts. The man turned and sniffed the air. He stepped over the woman's body before taking off and running straight for where Joseph and his siblings were hiding.

Joseph felt his sister shaking behind him. He braced himself as the man's legs came into view. He heard heavy breathing as the hunter stood against the backdrop of flames cascading towards the sky. Joseph felt the man bend towards the brush and sniff. He pushed out the machete just as the distant sound of another coyote yelp tinged the air. The hunter stopped, stood up, and took off in the direction of the sound.

Joseph did not resume breathing until the man's silhouette faded into the flames. He looked back at his brother and sister holding each other in the darkness. He crawled over and wrapped them in his embrace.

"*Kaka* is here."

*****

Joseph pulled a fish from the river and gutted it quickly. He watched Iyana nurse the fire while his younger brother picked flowers from the field a few feet away.

"Thomas!" Joseph yelled.

The tiny boy ran towards the makeshift camp. He gave Joseph the herbs and flowers before sitting down next to his sister at the fire. The two watched Joseph scale the fish and place small pieces on twigs. He handed each one a portion. The three sat in silence; the occasional sizzle of flesh the only sound between them.

Suddenly, Joseph jumped up and stood very still.

"What is it, *Kaka*?" Iyana asked quietly.

"Run towards the bushes." Joseph hissed. "*Now!*"

Izzy grabbed her baby brother's hand and bolted towards the tall brush. She crouched in silence watching Joseph walk the length of their tiny camp with his small machete against his thigh. He strolled to the edge of the brush and listened. He'd heard footsteps, he was sure of it. He turned at the sound of a twig breaking, machete at the ready. Hearing additional noises, Joseph plunged through the brush and hit the ground hard at his father's feet. The man picked up his son and hugged him.

"*Mwana*! You have made me proud."

Joseph could not comprehend the scene. It had been four days. He was uncertain he'd ever see his parents again, and here they stood in front of him. He dropped the machete and ran towards his mother, burying his face in the cloth covering her bulging belly. The woman's tears stained his face as she peppered it with kisses.

"*Mwana! Mwana.*"

"Where are your siblings?" Father asked.

"Iyana. *Kaka*. Come. Father and Mother are here," Joseph bellowed from his mother's arms.

Joseph heard his sister and brother's giggles as their father took them in his arms. Father cradled Iyana against his chest while bouncing Thomas on his lap. Joseph watched but did not move from his mother's arms. Instead, he nuzzled into the warmth of her embrace, inhaling her scent.

"I was afraid, Mama. I was afraid I would never see you again."

Joseph's mother cradled his face in her hands and kissed his forehead.

"Do not worry, my brave boy. You are blessed, *Mwana*. Yours is a story of many journeys. Do not be afraid."

*****

Joseph sat in the back of the jeep watching dark plumes of smoke rise against the horizon. The wispy spirals heralded the purges executed by the military to punish villagers that did not pay the appropriate ransoms, leaving the farmers without food for their livestock and little else to survive.

The family had traveled for two days along the hidden trails Joseph's father and uncle used to hunt. Many of these thoroughfares were abandoned or annexed by the military. Most people did not travel without permissions, and the routes were especially treacherous if you were unable to pay.

Joseph had worried for his mother as they'd trekked across the landscape. She was eight months pregnant and had recently been placed on bed rest. Several times, Joseph noticed the way his father walked next to his mother, wrapping his arm around her almost to carry her, as if he too, feared for her health. Yet she'd proven resilient; traversing the miles to the derelict farmstead where Joseph's uncle had hidden the beat up jeep.

Joseph rewound the past four days' chain of events. His mind heavy with revelations with which a nine-year-old child should never be burdened. His thoughts hovered around how much his parents had sacrificed. Abdicating their ancestries, depleting his mother's dowry, leaving their lives hoping to escape to a safer existence. But was there such a place? Was anywhere anodyne?

Joseph had once believed there was. He'd thought his life had been spared the turmoil he'd heard in whispered conversations. The fear he'd seen in his classmates as they left school each day. Fathers that had been killed, brothers that were soldiers, sisters who'd been violated or sacrificed to barter their family's safety. Joseph knew these circumstances weren't rational, yet they were a part of his existence; a fragment he desperately wanted to remove. He closed his eyes and struggled to quiet his thoughts; his mind shifting to the remnants of another's existence in time.

*****

Adam
Charleston, South Carolina

Adam pulled the mule over to the water trough and plopped down heavily on the ground next to the animal. He'd been in the fields since sunrise. His hands felt raw from holding the reins, and his legs did not seem to want to hold his weight. He heard the animal drinking heavily, a sign that he, too, was tired from the day's labor.

Adam pulled himself up beside the donkey and pushed his head under the surface of the water. He ignored the animal's protest and allowed the water to cover his head and ears. It was cool against his hot skin and felt good under the heat of the midday sun.

Adam relinquished his spot in time to see the headmaster's son strolling from the barn followed by one of the housemaids. The boy was a tiny replica of his father and just as mean. Adam watched him adjust his clothing and button his shirt as he turned to walk back towards the main house.

Adam quickly pulled the donkey away from the trough and back towards the field. He waited anxiously for any sound or indication that he'd been seen. As he hitched the animal back to the plow, he watched the young girl walk over to the trough and fill a bucket with water. She moved slowly towards the cover of the trees, sat the bucket down and began to undress. Picking the bucket up, she dumped the contents over her naked frame and began scrubbing vigorously with a pile of leaves, moving from her hair to her feet and back as if possessed. Adam watched in fascination as she retrieved the remaining water and poured it over her head as well, washing away her previous efforts. The girl quickly dressed and picked up the bucket. She looked around before turning and running towards the fields.

Aunt Mable had warned him to stay clear of such scenes. She'd told him on more than one occasion to disappear whenever he saw *bwana* [masters]. Despite his obedience, Adam was not afraid, but he'd witnessed his kinsmen beaten and maimed for defying the *bwana*. His uncle Abraham had thrashed several of the headmaster's farmhands who'd attempted to brand him with a cow iron. In turn, the headmaster had kidnapped Abraham, taken him to the river, whipped him with chicken wire, and left his body to rot on the spikes by the waterwheel. Several of the homestead's male slaves had risked their lives to bring Abraham home. All of them had been beaten for the deed, but Mable and the other women had taken care of their wounds and nursed them back to health. Abraham never recovered; he'd died from an infection.

Despite several suitors, Mable had not remarried and had raised Adam and her two sons alone. If it had not been for his family, Adam would have run. He knew the woods and the rivers from the maps Abraham had drawn for him. He knew the way to freedom was north of the mouth of the river.

Adam finished strapping the donkey into the harness. He jumped on the plow and gave the reins a swift snap. The animal bolted into stride, jerking the plow into motion. Adam held on, steering the animal around the field, watching the sun settle against the sky. He strained to imagine what the world was like on the other side of that ball of fire. Freedom sounded foreign in his native Swahili, but he remembered it as the last word his uncle had uttered before closing his eyes in eternal rest.

*****

Matthew sat across from his mother attempting to thread a needle. The boy positioned the thread between his fingers, picked up the tiny object, and held it steady in front of his face. He closed one eye, as he'd seen his mother do several times, and moved his fingers slowly towards the needle's center. He pushed the thread towards the opening, pulled, and cursed, realizing he'd missed.

"Watch yo mouth, boy," Mable snapped.

"Yes'm."

Sensing her son's frustration, Mable picked up a needle, licked her fingers, kneaded the thread between them and pushed the fiber through the eye. She handed the apparatus to her son and returned to her stitching.

"Don't fret. You'll get it." She smiled at the child.

Matthew smiled before picking up the wad of material he'd been working with. Mable watched his hands move along the seams. She smiled at the thought of redoing the stiches while he slept and replacing the fabric at the foot of his bed. His efforts wanted it to be a scarf, and a scarf it would be. She smiled and resumed her reflections concerning the rest of her day.

Adam was in the fields. Elijah, her youngest, was with her brother, hunting for winter meat and supplies. She'd kept Matthew home to monitor his illness. She was not overly concerned but cautious. Everyone in the Big House was sick, and Mable did not want to risk the malady rearing its head among her neighbors, having lost several good souls to such the year prior.

Mable rose from the table and walked towards the pot of stew bubbling on the stove. She stirred the fragrant brew and bent to lower the fire, peeking at the cake rising in the oven. It was Adam's birthday, and the sweets were a surprise.

Turning back towards Matthew, Mable stopped. The headmasters' oldest son, Kaleb, was standing in the doorway watching her. From nowhere, a *bwana* stormed into the room and grabbed Matthew by his shirt. Mable picked up her blade and moved forward.

"Stop right there, woman," the *bwana* hissed. "Why ain't this boy in the fields?"

Mable kept her voice calm despite her fear. "He sick, boss. Fever and a bad stomach."

"He looks fine to me." The man took Matthew by the neck and shook the child violently.

Mable felt the butt of the blade dig into her flesh. She moved her eyes from the man standing in the doorway to the one holding her son. She locked eyes with Matthew, hoping to assuage his fears.

"You dat whore married to the nigger Daddy whipped at the river."

Mable felt her blood boil at the mention of her husband.

"That was more than five years ago." Kaleb sneered as he looked Mable up and down. "Long time for a woman to be without a man."

Mable saw something in the man's eyes she'd seen too many times while working at the Big House in the bayou. She cradled the blade against her palm and felt the wetness of blood on its tip. She watched as Kaleb addressed the *bwana* holding her son.

"Take the boy to the barn with the others." Turning back towards Mable, he smiled. "Me and his Mammy gonna reminisce about her husband."

The *bwana* pushed Matthew towards the door. Matthew kicked the man across the shin and ran towards his mother. Pushing the boy behind her with one hand, Mable pushed the blade up and out with the other catching the *bwana's* upper arm with the brunt of the blade. The man screamed, reaching for the gaping cut along his bicep. Cursing, Kaleb moved from the door and stepped between them. He punched Mable in the gut and bent her hand backwards, forcing her to drop the blade before snatching Matthew from her grip and pushing the boy towards a second man that appeared from the yard.

"The two of you is dumber than dirt. Go over to the house and take care of that arm. Finish making the rounds of the remaining cabins and get to the barn."

The two men exited the doorway leaving Kaleb behind. Mable heard Matthew scream and then the air went silent. She forced her way up off the floor and tried to move pass Kaleb but he pushed her backwards towards the small bed in the corner.

"Daddy said your man never uttered a word; even when they splayed his skin open with chicken wire. He wasn't sure if it was because he was unconscious or mute. Didn't matter which. When they took the shears to his crotch, that's when they got a yell from him."

Mable felt the sting of tears behind her eyes, but she willed them away. She refused to bend to this bastard no matter what he did to her. He had a weathered look with a slim, tawny frame; dead eyes and a line of rotting teeth around his bottom lip probably from chewing tobacco. In confirmation, Kaleb spewed a mouthful of the venom across the floor and wiped his chin as he moved towards her.

Kaleb shifted towards the stove and picked up a fork. He pushed the utensil into the flame and watched the edges blacken. He turned the object round and round before pulling it free and looking towards Mable.

"When I was 'bout your boy's age, Daddy would take me with him to the slave quarters. I'd sit in the doorway while he did his business. Trousers around his ankles, grunting like he was riding a horse. No matter when Daddy came, the whores would just lay there. Never saw one fight back." Kaleb smiled. "You ain't like them, is ya?"

He reached for Mable. She grabbed the frying pan and swung; feeling metal hit bone, she felt a flicker of hope. Kaleb staggered backwards dazed but kept coming. Mable reached for the pot of stew, but he pulled her away, pushed her onto the floor and began kicking her repeatedly. When he was spent, he stepped back. Mable lay curled in a fetal position, breathing heavily. Kaleb moved forward, pulled her off the floor by the nape of her neck and tossed her onto the bed. Moving towards her, he noticed the blade she'd used. He picked it up smiling.

"You ain't nothing like them at all."

*****

"Auntie!" Adam yelled from the yard.

He waited for a response but received none; the hair on the back of his neck tingled. The evening sun was disappearing behind the trees. The soft glow cast an eerie light on the entrance to the house. Normally, his younger brothers would be in the yard playing. His aunt's singing would greet him at the top of the hill. Today. Nothing. No one moved.

Adam eased into the doorway. The smell of burnt food pierced his nostrils. As his eyes adjusted to the shades, he saw his aunt lying half naked on the bed. He made his way towards her but stopped short at the fierceness in her voice.

"Stay away."

Mable moved slowly off the bed; pulling her dress over her frame as she rose. Her motions appeared painful and deliberate. She turned towards Adam and his heart stopped. Mable's face was tattered and bloody; one eye swollen shut, the other badly bruised. Her lip was torn; scratches and bite marks visible across her chest.

"Auntie! Who did this? Where are Matthew and Elijah?"

"The *bwana* took the young ones." Mable winced. "Go to your uncle's. It's not safe."

"I won't go without you."

"Hear me, boy!" Mable's voice shook. "This ain't no place for you no more. That bastard's Daddy is evil even from the grave. He took my husband. He won't have my children."

"What about you?"

Mable smiled. Her swollen lips curling around her bloody teeth.

"I'mma be. Find my boys."

Mable staggered and fell. Adam hurried to her side, but she swatted him away with a strength he could not fathom existed in the woman kneeling before him.

"Leave me!"

Mable slowly pushed up from the floor. She stood and pulled her dress straight; smoothing the dirty fabric between her fingers. She stared at Adam before moving towards him. She laid her hands on his shoulders. Adam trembled with rage as tears rolled down his cheeks. Mable reached up and wiped them away.

"I have loved you like my child since they took my sister from me." She smiled, the crow's feet framing the sadness in her eyes. "Go! Use what Abraham showed you to find the trails. Lead my boys to *uhuru* [freedom]."

Mable pulled Adam close and held him. He reluctantly returned her embrace, afraid he'd hurt her, but his fear subsided as he listened to her hum softly. When she released him, Adam felt the chill from the evening air swirl between them. Mable turned her back to him and walked towards the bed. She sat down and lowered her head as Adam had seen her do oftentimes to pray.

"Leave me, Adam. Go to your uncle's. Find your brothers. Keep them safe."

Mable lay down on the bed and closed her eyes. Adam tried to speak but could only stand in the darkness crying. He willed himself to move, turning towards the door of the cabin. He paused and looked towards his auntie. She did not move. Adam whispered a silent prayer and ran. He jogged through the forest along the familiar trails his uncle had shown him until he reached a large tree at the edge of the river. He began to climb. When he pulled up onto the ledge of the tree house he'd built, he sat down and wept.

Eventually, the tears subsided, and Adam began preparing for the day-long journey to his uncle's. He packed the hunting knife he'd fashioned from an elk's horn and the slingshot Abraham had made for him. He moved through the space as if expecting an intruder. He stopped and listened to the wind; thunder in the distance. He'd have to move quickly to cross the river before the storm. Adam considered waiting, but a sense of urgency captured the thought. He pulled the coon knapsack over his head and scaled the trunk to the ground below. A slow mist covered his face and arms as he moved through the trees. He picked up his pace and focused on moving and a plan of action once he'd retrieved Elijah. The main goal was finding Matthew. Adam hoped he could do so before the auctions, or he feared his brother would be lost.

I will find him, Auntie. Ahadi [promise].

*****

Adam arrived at his uncle's cabin during the evening. His aunt was preparing dinner and had been startled by his sudden appearance at her door. She knew from his demeanor that something had transpired, but despite her cues, Adam would not divulge the reason for his visit.

Perplexed, she placed a bowl of hot stew before him and returned to tending the baby lying in the middle of the bed. Adam watched the woman open her blouse and gently prompt the four-month-old baby girl to feed. The child's tiny hand curled in a tight fist, bounced through the air seemingly in tune with her mother's singing.

Adam did not speak but merely sat and stared out the window towards the fields where his kinsman toiled with thoughts of the meager comforts of their families to return to. He rose when he saw his uncle and Elijah moving down the road towards the cabin. He walked the short distance to meet them, embraced Elijah, and gestured to his uncle that he needed to speak with him.

"Go on to the cabin, Elijah. Adam and me going to the barn to prep the horses."

"Imma come too."

"Elijah. Do as Uncle say."

Elijah looked from his uncle to Adam and back. His mind knew something was not right, but he'd been told to go and he knew not to disobey. Reluctantly, he turned and continued the trek to his uncle's cabin.

"Why you here, boy?" Adam's uncle sat on a bale of hay and plucked a straw free. He popped off the tip and stuck the clean end between his teeth.

"I come for Elijah."

"He staying with me while Mable get the Big House ready for the winter. Ain't no need for you to take him."

Adam's Uncle saw a shadow move across Adam's face. "What's done happened, Adam?"

Adam looked away, afraid the anger in his gut would manifest in tears.

"Answer me, boy!"

"The *bwana* took Matthew. They hurt Auntie. She made me leave."

Adam's uncle spat the hay out and stood; the girth of his 6'4", 250-pound frame filling the space between them.

"You ain't leavin' to go nowhere. If the *bwana* took Matthew, likely he already gone. Mable wants ya safe, and I intend to keep you that way."

Adam felt the air in his lungs tighten as he opened his mouth to speak. "Auntie made me promise to take them over the trails."

"Adam. You can't go back. They likely lookin' for ya."

Adam looked up at his uncle and swallowed the anger in his throat.

"Elijah and I leavin' in da morning. I promised Auntie I'd find Matthew. I intend to."

Adam's uncle watched him walk away. He knew what the boy would find when he returned to the homestead. He knew his sister better than anyone, and if she'd sent him away, he knew she'd done so to protect him. He also knew Adam was as stubborn as his mother, Mable's baby sister. The boy's mind was set, and there was nothing that was going to keep him from honoring Mable's request.

*****

Adam and Elijah walked through the woods slowly. The air was moist and heavy; occasional bursts of lightning illuminated the landscape, casting shadows on the trees. Adam moved cautiously. His uncle had warned of frequent raids and had advised Adam take the route through the forest on the other side of the stream adjacent to the homestead. The trip had taken an extra day, but he and Elijah had not encountered any of the slave catchers.

Adam rounded the corner and stopped; smoke rose from the burnt shell of his aunt's cabin. Despite the heavy rain, the debris smoldered against the dark sky. Anger boiled from his core. His mind twisted in knots by a loathing his sixteen-year-old psyche could barely contain. He looked away from the remains propped against the far wall; tattered scraps of his aunt's dress fluttered against the breeze.

The clouds parted from the moon, causing the heavy raindrops to shimmer as they hit the horizon. Elijah stood behind him, crying. Adam could offer no comfort. The child had lost his mother. Adam had lost the only woman he'd ever known as such. Everything he knew about the world was shattered, yet Mabel had asked him to find hope for Elijah and Matthew. Why hadn't she stayed to guide him?

Adam pulled Elijah close and looked into his tiny face. "We need to keep moving. Do you understand?"

Elijah wiped his face and nodded. Adam raised his eyes towards the sky before taking a final look towards his Aunt's remains.

"*Kwaheri* [goodbye], Auntie."

Adam struggled to move past the scene and focus on finding Matthew. The auctions occurred fifty miles from the headmaster's ranch. The *bwana* were on horseback with wagons and a day's head start. He and Elijah would have to move through the forest on foot to continue to avoid the raids. Adam intended to follow the creeks to

Shepherd's Inn, the last stop before the Old Slave Mart. He'd figure out the rest when they got there. For now, he needed to find food and a warm place for them to rest. Elijah wouldn't be able to keep up much longer. Adam turned to look at the eight-year-old boy behind him. Elijah had no idea where they were going or what was going to happen, but Adam knew he would do whatever he asked without question.

They stopped at the edge of the river. The rain sounded like gunshots bouncing through the trees. In the clearing, Adam saw a black spot against the landscape, a cave. He moved slowly towards the entrance, keeping his eyes trained for any movement or indication of danger. He reached behind him to pull Elijah closer. As the child moved under his brother's arm, Adam sensed movement to his left. He turned to see a raccoon scurrying into the brush. He released his breath and stopped. He picked up a large rock and tossed it into the belly of the structure, bracing himself. Anything present would come out quickly. He tried again and waited. Nothing. It appeared to be empty. He took Elijah's hand and led him inside.

"We'll stay here for the night."

Elijah moved deeper into the cave and settled next to a bundle of rocks. Adam stood in the entrance watching him. Elijah pushed a handful of dirt into a mound and proceeded to place rocks and twigs around it. Adam had seen his uncle Abraham perform the task many times during their hunting trips. He felt an acute sadness at the familiarity of watching Elijah move in the same manner.

"Do not leave the cave. I won't be far."

Adam turned and eased into the downpour of rain. The best opportunity for food was the river, but it would be dangerous. The runoff from the rain was causing the water to move quickly; one slip would send him downstream towards the falls. Adam turned over several rocks, looking for trapped fish and dormant frogs. He cut a swatch of blueberries from an adjacent vine. It wasn't much, but it would keep them moving.

He made his way back to the cave. Moving up the path, he saw a soft glow emanating from the entrance. He entered the cave from the darkest side, slowly making his way along the wall; careful not to make a sound. He heard the crackle of the fire growing louder. As he rounded the corner, he saw his younger brother sitting bare chested with his shirt twisted on a makeshift spike next to the flames.

"Elijah."

The boy turned and smiled with a huge grin.

"I wanted to surprise you. I remember how Papa told us to make the fire small so the smoke is harder to see. I found some fire rocks deeper in the cave and used them on a piece of my trousers and the skin from this." The boy moved to reveal a long, skinned snake roasting across the small fire. "He was coiled up under the rocks by the entrance."

Adam smiled.

"Did I do okay?"

"Yes, Elijah. You have done well. Papa would be very proud of you. Here." Adam tossed the items he'd collected to his brother. "Dry these out."

Elijah pulled out his pocket knife and began scaling the fish. Adam watched the boy work; concentrating like he'd seen his aunt do many times preparing dinner. The picture of Mable's broken frame creased his memory.

Adam suddenly felt tired. He sat down next to the fire and tried to contain the anguish teasing the edge of his thoughts. He had no idea if Matthew was alive. If they found him, he had no clue how they were going to make it across the border to the system of trails his uncle had shown him. He barely knew what to do next, and yet he had to be strong for Elijah. His aunt's words floated across his heart.

"I promised you I'd take care of them, Auntie. I swear on my life; I will find a way."

*****

Adam lay on his back listening to the sounds within the cave. His instincts told him it was barely 5:00 a.m. Elijah lay huddled against the rocks. The fire he'd built smoked in the pit next to them. Adam sat up and tossed a handful of dirt towards the pile. The hiss made him stop momentarily. He'd heard something. Looking down at his brother, he moved away quietly.

He scuttled against the wall and peaked out a small enclosure highlighted by the rising sun. As his eyes adjusted, Adam saw a large black bear advancing towards the cave. The animal was a few feet away but directly in view of where he and Elijah would have to exit. To make matters worse, Adam saw two small cubs bouncing in the brush behind her. A black bear was dangerous; a mama black bear was deadly.

Adam crawled over to Elijah and shook the child awake. He quickly silenced the boy and hastened him to get dressed. Adam searched the cave for anything that could be used as a distraction. He spotted the dried fish Elijah had prepared. It upset him to have to use their supply of food, but it would have to work. He and Elijah quickly assembled their wares and moved towards the mouth of the cave.

Adam saw the bears in the underbrush near the blueberry bush. He took his slingshot and loaded the fish. Pulling the leather backwards, he let it fly over the bears head. He watched the animal sniff the air before returning to the berries. Adam cursed softly but then watched as the animal slowly turned in the direction of the fish. He pulled Elijah close. As the mother bear moved towards the direction of the scent, Adam and Elijah eased out of the cave and around the enclosure to the wet grass surrounding the rocks. They took off running, cleared the wooded area, and came to a small valley. Breathless and wet, the two squatted in the shade of a large tree. Nothing stirred. There was no indication that the family had picked up their scent. Adam pushed a thankful prayer towards the heavens and rose with Elijah to continue their journey.

*****

Cayce, South Carolina

Adam watched the *bwana* bounce in and out the side entrance while unloading the wagon. He shifted to get a better look around the building and spotted the group of boys tied to a tree next to the horses. Surveying the landscape, Adam saw a small bale of hay located across from the trees which would be his best opportunity for getting closer to them.

The men moved around the wagon quickly; the lightning and thunder overhead promising a heavy storm. As if on cue, the wind picked up and Adam felt moisture around his nostrils. He would use the rain as cover, but he needed something to cut the chains restraining the boys. He turned to Elijah.

"Do you see the store on the other side of the road? I need an ax, the biggest you can carry. When you get it, meet me on the other side of that bale of hay. Can you do that?"

The child shook his head affirmatively and moved away from his brother.

Adam watched Elijah move around the barn and across the street to the store. He saw the boy's silhouette linger a moment at the window before disappearing into the building. Adam said a silent prayer and moved away from the bushes.

He made his way towards the back of the inn. Peeking through a small window, he saw the *bwana* seated at a table near the bar. Adam watched two barmaids settle next to them. One of the men grabbed the woman closest to him and violently pulled her onto his lap before pushing his hand under her dress. The woman smiled awkwardly before placing her hands around his neck. Adam hoped the *bwana* remained occupied while he attempted to free the others. He moved away from the window towards the wagon.

Adam climbed into the back of the vehicle. There were a few bags of rice, a pouch of dried meat, and a length of rope. He wrapped the rope around his shoulder followed by the pouch and then cut a small hole into one of the bags. Using his shirt, he filled the garment with rice, tied it in several knots and twisted the arms around his waist. He looked towards the store and watched as Elijah carried a large ax over to the bale of hay. Adam slid down from the wagon and turned to make his way to Elijah.

Rounding the corner, he spotted a man approaching from the opposite direction. Adam stopped dead in his tracks. He watched the man move along the path towards the tree where the boys were tied. The man stopped, unzipped his trousers and peed before moving towards the inn. Adam caught him midstride, tripped him from behind and quickly cracked the rim around his skull with a large rock. The man lay still. Adam waited in the darkness for any movement. When nothing stirred, he dragged the unconscious man towards the barn. He quickly undressed the man, confiscated the knife and few dollars he had in his pockets before gagging and tying him to one of the horse stalls.

Adam exited the barn to pouring rain and sprinted towards the bale of hay. Untying the rice and removing the pouch, he tied both around Elijah's waist before taking the ax and moving towards the trees. Adam quickly walked around the group from child to child. He breathed a sigh of relief when he saw Matthew huddled next to one of the larger boys on the far side.

"I need y'all to move closer together," Adam whispered against the sound of the rain.

The boys scooted towards each other. Adam lifted the ax and waited. As a loud clap of thunder filled the air, he let the ax fall. He heard the links crack, but they did not break. He lifted the instrument again and waited. Looking beyond the rain, he saw one of the *bwana* exit the inn. Adam moved into the shadows and waited. The man looked up towards the sky. He shifted his weight and turned his head towards the tree where the boys were chained. Adam did not move. The man stared a long time. He turned but stopped and looked inside the bar. He took another look towards the tree before turning to go back into the inn.

Adam resumed breathing. He moved back into position and raised the ax to prepare for another strike. As the thunder clapped, he let the ax fall once again. He felt the blow loosen the chain's grip. He watched the boys rise. Gathering them together, he pushed them towards the woods. He hugged Matthew quickly before pushing him to join the others. Adam picked up the youngest of the group and placed the child onto his back before joining the others in the underbrush.

"Stay close. Hold on to each other if you have to."

One by one, the boys passed Adam moving into the interior. He turned back towards the inn. Nothing stirred. Adam switched directions and worked his way back to the horses. He untied the reins, careful not to spook them; the thunder would take care of that. As he loosened the last of the ropes, Adam grabbed the arms of the little one on his back and made his way towards the forest. He looked at the sky; the rain pounded the earth like a metallic drum. He prayed it would give them a head start and cover their tracks. He'd accomplished the hardest task; now all he had to do was lead them through the forest and across the river to what he hoped would be a better life.

*****

Adam stood at the bank of the river watching the water rush by. He and the boys had been moving through the forest for hours. The rain had finally stopped but not before creating fast-moving rapids and strong currents along the river.

Adam pulled the rope from the wagon around his waist; he tugged to ensure the other end was securely wrapped around the adjacent tree. He turned to look at the small group of boys. They were various ages; most had never been away from the homestead, yet here they stood waiting for him to lead them into the unknown. He walked over to Matthew and Elijah.

"I want the two of you to go across first. Y'all remember the paths Papa taught us? Just over that ridge, you gonna find one. If anything happens, stay on that path. Don't stop for nothing or nobody. Keep going till you reach the house Uncle showed us in the picture book. Do y'all remember?"

The two boys shook their heads. Adam took each in his arms and held them close. He rubbed his hand over the top of their heads and smiled to ease the tension he felt. When they smiled back, he saw his auntie's face in each of theirs. He turned away quickly.

He stepped off the bank into the cold, fast-moving water. He pulled the rope again to ensure it was tight and quickly waded across the river. The water was shallow, but the current was strong. As he moved into the middle, the water rose to his chest. As he got closer to the shore, it moved to his waist. Adam worried the smaller boys would not be able to withstand the current. He'd have to go back to get them. He motioned for Matthew and Elijah to come across.

Adam watched Matthew step off first and reach back for Elijah's hand. Matthew held on to the rope with one hand and guided Elijah along with the other. Adam felt proud and afraid simultaneously as he watched them traverse the river bottom. At one point, Matthew slipped and went under. Adam sprang forward but stopped as he saw him fight to his feet and continue to hold Elijah. When they'd made it to the other side, Adam hugged them tightly before stepping off to guide the next set of boys.

Adam grabbed two more boys. He repeated this until he'd gotten all of them across. He placed the youngest on the ground and gave him a shove towards the forest. As he stepped near the bank, he saw a flash of light from the interior; the omen he'd been dreading. He pulled Matthew close, signaling for the boy to be quiet.

"I need y'all to get movin'."

Matthew looked up at his brother with fear. "What about you? I'm not leaving you."

"The *bwana* are on the other side of the clearing. Without the rain, we have no cover. We have to depend on darkness. You can lead them the rest of the way. Follow the river. They don't know where we've gone just yet. If I keep them on the wrong path, y'all can get away."

"I won't go without you."

Adam shook the ten-year-old boy with both hands.

"Listen to me, *Kaka*! I will catch up. I need you to be strong. Papa will guide you. Now go!"

Matthew wrapped his arms around Adam before pushing away to move towards Elijah and the others. He briefly addressed the group and then turned towards the forest. Adam watched them disappear into the thicket. He saw Elijah stop and turn back before Matthew gently pulled him to follow the others.

In the distance, Adam saw the small flicker of light again. Moving away from the shore, he quietly waded back into the water. He pulled up, cut the rope from the tree and wrapped it around his chest. Using a pile of wet branches, he erased their footprints from the bank and tossed the leaves into the current. He squatted behind a patch of rocks and listened, waiting for the steady punch of horse hooves and the occasional whisper.

Adam moved along the river until he'd made it to an open clearing. The water was slower because of the rocks so he was able to skirt over them quickly. He hopped up on the shore and waited. In the distance, he saw three men on horseback appear. Adam moved further into the thicket and began running. As he made his way through the trees, he heard the *bwana* shouting.

"Over that way. See the movement in the trees. The birds. Follow the birds."

Adam moved quickly. His feet flying over the wet ground as he followed the course of the river towards the falls. He could hear the thunder of the falls getting louder as he pushed on. Behind him, he heard the pitter of the horses as they moved through the trees. He had an advantage because the trees were tightly knit and the ground was wet. The *bwana* would have to be careful for fear of injuring the horses.

"Do you see him? Where did he go? Over there. Down near the ridge. See the tracks. He's moving through the trees. We need to flush him out. Damn horses can't keep up. Get my gun. Where's my gun? I got a view. I can take him."

Adam kept moving. He pushed past a large oak tree and moved in front of it, keeping his body in line with the tree's shadow. He jumped over roots and flew past bushes. The *bwana* were a whisper against the wind in his ears as he continued to run. Ahead of him, he saw the dim light from the clearing. The roar of the water was deafening as he burst free from the thicket. He stopped at the edge and looked out over the falls. The water cascaded down into a cloud of foam and fog below.

Adam looked around him. There was nothing. He couldn't go back. He looked to his right and saw a cluster of bushes. He jumped the small cliff and hit the rocks hard, banging his knee. He lay still allowing the pain to roll across his mind. He stood up and immediately buckled over from the pain. He could hear the men shouting on the other side of the trees.

Adam stood up and gingerly placed his leg on the ground. It resisted the weight, but he continued to force it down until his foot was on the ground. He limped towards the bushes. The numbness in his leg gave him a bit of lift. He pushed down and powered his way around the bushes into the dense underbrush. Gritting his teeth, he forced himself into a trot. He moved as fast as he could through the bushes until he'd come to a system of caves. He didn't have time to check which might be occupied. He said a silent prayer and moved towards the smaller of the openings. He pushed his way inside.

It was damp and dark. Adam pressed further into the cave and stopped on a bed of rocks shadowed from the interior. He rolled up his pants leg and touched the swollen flesh around his knee cap. It wasn't broken, but it was definitely sprained. He cut a small piece of rope and a portion of his shirt and wrapped his knee. He stood up and felt the pain run through his system, but the leg did not give way. Adam closed his eyes and filtered out the steady hum of water, the rhythmic drone of the crickets and cicadae. In the background, he could hear the *bwana* shouting in the distance.

"Did they jump? Kincaid's not gonna be happy if they've jumped. That's a month's worth of feed."

"Stop talking and let me think. Bring me one of the lanterns."

Adam moved further into the cave. As he pushed into the darkness, he felt a breeze caress his cheek. He held up his head and let the moisture settle. There was an opening somewhere on the other side of the wall. He placed his hand against the wall as a guide in the darkness and continued to move. As he limped through the cavern, the roar of the falls faded replaced with that of a gentler flowing stream. He shifted around a set of large boulders and entered a wider enclosure. Adam walked over to the large stream and knelt down for a drink. He cupped his hand and let the water run through his fingers. It felt clean. He stuck his nose into the palm of his hand like his Uncle had taught him. Sticking his head under the water, he saw fish and turtles. The water was cold. He pushed up and waded into it up to his waist. The cool liquid felt good around his swollen knee. Taking a deep breath, Adam went under and began swimming towards the opening on the far end. He pushed past rocks and reefs, marveled at the colorful fish swimming away from him. He came up for air and surveyed his surroundings. He was in a smaller cave. The opening was closer, but he had a few more feet to swim. He went back under the surface and continued to push forward.

Adam came up and pushed onto the bank. He eased his weight onto his good leg and gently forced the other to follow. It was becoming stiff and harder to move, but he could not afford to stop. As he moved through the trees, he heard a loud boom and felt a swift puff of wind move across his left side.

Adam did not turn to see where the shot originated. He ignored the pain in his knee and pushed as fast as he could through the trees. He felt another puff of wind. He shifted to his right around a large tree and continued to move. As he came upon another clearing, he felt a sharp pain in his thigh and another in his right arm. Adam screamed, but he would not stop. As he continued to move, he felt an explosion of pain in his left leg. He tumbled to the ground and came to rest next to a patch of dandelions. He thought of Matthew and Elijah as his vision dimmed.

"Watch over them, Auntie."

*****

Adam woke up with the tail of a mule in his face. He tried to push himself up but couldn't move his hands. He lay still a moment. His head bounced in rhythm with the mule's motion. He pushed up again and was able to shift his weight. He moved several times and finally managed to move away from the mule's tail. Adam lay across the animal's back listening. The pain in his left leg was excruciating. His right arm was stiff, and his head was full of cotton. He felt sick; the smell of horse manure and wet grass overwhelmed his senses.

He coughed and felt the bile rise in his throat. He regurgitated; his stomach retched, pushing the vile liquid from his system. Adam breathed in heavily trying to stave off another bout of nausea.

"The Negra's awake."

Adam heard the *bwana* on the other side of him. He was too weak to lift his head. His stomach continued to churn as another bout of vomiting shook his frame.

"Damn bastard's throwing up all over the horse."

"No matter. We're almost to the clearing. Looks like there's a house ahead. We'll stop for provisions."

Adam lay still praying his head would stop spinning. His stomach muscles continued to flex, attempting to purge the infection from his system. He felt the fever rising from his leg. He tried to move it and couldn't. He closed his eyes and tried not to panic.

"Hello! Anyone home? We're looking for fresh horses and something hot to eat."

Elizabeth and her husband, Lee, stood in the back of the kitchen watching the men approach their house.

"I'm going out to talk to them. You make sure the boys stay quite."

Lee kissed his wife and moved away from her side out the kitchen door. She watched him for a moment before moving into the other room. She waited before getting down on her knees and crawling under the dining room table. She lifted a small door. Lying down on her belly, she placed her feet on the top rung of the ladder and eased her way down. She moved quickly down the ladder into the semidarkened space. As she turned to face the room, she saw the tiny, scared faces of the seven boys looking back at her.

"I need you all to be very quiet. The *bwana* are here."

Matthew turned to the other boys and back towards the woman.

"Is my brother with them?"

"I don't know."

Matthew got up from the floor and moved towards her.

"Where are you going?"

"To see if Adam is with them."

Elizabeth moved towards him in a panic.

"You can't. They'll know you're here. They'll find you and take you to the auctions. You need to stay here with the other boys and keep quiet."

Matthew continued to move towards the ladder.

"No." Elizabeth moved between him and the ladder. "Young man? Did you hear me?"

"Yes, ma'am. But I need to see my brother."

Elizabeth looked at the child. He had such a look of conviction and determination, she knew she could not stop him. She stepped aside and watched him scale the ladder. After a few moments, she followed, leaving the remaining children huddled together in the darkness.

Matthew made his way to the far window. He peeked out over the ledge into the yard. He saw the *bwana* and Lee standing near the barn. He left the window and made his way to the back end of the house. He pushed out the door and into the backyard. Crawling through the bushes, he made his way around the yard to the side of the barn. He entered from the horses' stall, climbed up to the loft, and walked over to the window. Looking down into the yard, he saw the *bwana* talking while Lee pushed hay towards the horses. Matthew's heart leapt into his throat when he saw Adam's dirty frame tossed on the back of one of the mules. He swallowed hard, fighting the tears and anger.

Elizabeth joined her husband at the well. She'd brought out a basket of biscuits and a pitcher of water.

"You gentlemen interested in some warm biscuits and jam?"

"Thank you, ma'am. We appreciate that very much."

Elizabeth spotted Adam on the mule. She noted the tattered clothing and the bloody rags around his leg.

"That young man needs tending to. That leg looks infected."

"We only have a few miles to the auction house. He'll live."

Lee took note from his wife. He stopped moving the hay and turned to the headmaster.

"My wife's right. A healthy buck will fetch more than a half dead one. She's a nurse. I'm the town physician. We can fix him right up. He'll be considerably better by the time y'all make it to auction. At least, it'll break the fever."

The headmaster tossed the last of the biscuit in his mouth and took a large swig of the cold water. He was already pissed about losing the lot of boys. Taking a cut on an injured slave was not an ideal compromise.

"Cut him loose. Let Doc here tend to that leg."

"We'll lose an hour maybe two. We could miss the auction."

"Let me worry about the auction. Bradley ain't gonna shut down without talking to me first. Mr. Lee and Madame are offering the hospitality of their home. A hot meal and a few hours' rest won't matter."

One of the men cut Adam loose from the mule and let him slide onto the ground. Adam crumpled beneath the animal's belly and moaned. Elizabeth hesitated before moving slowly to his side. She placed the basket on the ground before lifting the tattered garment around Adam's leg. She gasped at the torn muscle and ligament protruding from his leg below the swollen knee cap.

"Move him into the barn. We need to stop the bleeding. Get some bandages. It needs to be cleaned and wrapped."

None of the men moved. Elizabeth looked up towards the headmaster, silently pleading. The man looked at her dismissively before shouting at two of his colleagues.

"Do as she says. Move him into the barn."

The men reluctantly pulled Adam off the ground and tossed him into one of the horse stalls. Elizabeth retrieved her basket and turned back towards the house.

"You gentlemen are welcome to come inside and wash up. I have some leftovers I can put together for you. Give you a good home-cooked meal to send you on your way."

Elizabeth looked towards Lee; he gave a slight nod. The men followed Elizabeth into the house. Lee waited a moment before moving towards the barn. When he entered the space, he saw Matthew huddled next to Adam.

"Son, you can't be here. They could come back at any moment. It's not safe."

Matthew looked up at Lee with tears in his eyes. He did not move. He bent down towards Adam and took his hand in his own.

"Adam. Can you hear me, *Kaka*?"

Adam heard the soft voice through a fog. He opened his eyes and felt the pain rush his senses. He lifted his hand and touched Matthew's face. He was weak, but he recognized his brother. He whispered softly, "Where's Elijah?"

"We found the house. Elijah and the others are inside."

Adam squeezed Matthew's hand and then tried to push him away.

"Go."

"I won't leave you. You're hurt."

Adam tried to sit up. Matthew moved beneath him and pulled him up into his arms.

"Leave me, *Kaka*. Please. I can't help you anymore. I promised Auntie. You must go."

Lee watched the boys with a sense of sadness. He leaned down and pulled Matthew away from Adam.

"Come on, son. You need to get out of here. Go back to the loft. Wait for me to come back. Hurry."

Matthew pulled away from Lee and wiped his face on his sleeve. He took one last look at Adam before moving away and scaling the ladder back to the loft. Lee watched him disappear into the shadows of the space.

Lee bent down next to Adam and assessed his wounds. His leg was badly damaged. He checked the bloodstained area around his arm. It was bloody but appeared to only be grazed and swollen. He lifted Adam's head and pushed a ladle of water towards him.

"Drink, son."

Adam gulped the water down hungrily. Lee filled the ladle and gave him another drink.

Elizabeth entered the barn quietly. She handed Lee his doctor's bag and a lantern.

"One of the children left the house."

"He's in the loft."

"Oh, thank the Lord." Lee saw Elizabeth physically relax.

"I don't know how much longer I can stall them."

Lee stood up. "Go in the pantry and pull out that bottle of Christmas whiskey Mrs. Davenport gave me last year. That should keep them busy while I patch him up."

Lee placed a light kiss on Elizabeth's cheek. He gave her a hug before releasing her and watching her make her way back to the house. He looked down at Adam and knelt by his side.

"I'm gonna take a look at that leg. It's gonna hurt like hell, but I don't have a choice."

Adam lay still. The water had curbed the nausea. He felt Lee moving around his left leg. When he touched the area around the bullet, Adam bit his tongue to curb the scream in his chest.

"Bullet's still in there. I gotta get that out or you'll lose the leg. Do you understand?"

Adam nodded his head. Lee grabbed a pair of pincers from the nearby stall. He poured alcohol over the edge before sticking them in the flame of the lantern. He stood up and positioned himself over Adam's frame. He eased down onto the boy's thighs to pin him down while he prepared to probe for the bullet.

"You ready, son?"

Lee did not wait for a response. He pushed the metal end of the pincers into Adam's leg. The walls shook with the ferocity of Adam's screams as Lee moved the pincer's against the bone within the wound trying to get a hold of the bullet's tail. He pushed his full weight down onto Adam's leg and gave the pincers a hard yank. The bullet came out clean. Lee assessed the area around the bone; it did not appear to be broken or splintered.

Adam lay unconscious in the stall. Lee touched his forehead and the area around his neck. Adam's breathing was erratic, but there was a steady pulse. Lee quickly went to work on cleaning the wound on Adam's arm and the area around his leg. He walked over to the farthest stall and retrieved one of the hay sacks. He cut the bag into long strips, doused each in the bucket of water several times before wetting them with alcohol and wrapping them around Adam's leg. Having stopped the bleeding, Lee turned his attention to Adam's swollen knee cap. He moved the appendage from side to side. It did not appear broken. He touched the puffy flesh around the joint. There did not appear to be any infection. He took another strip of cloth and wrapped the knee tightly. Lee checked Adam's forehead again. The fever seemed to be breaking. Hopefully, that meant the infection had not leaked into his bloodstream. Lee stood up and looked up towards the loft.

"Your brother's going to be okay. I'm going back to the house. I'll come and get you when it's safe. I need you to stay up there and out of sight."

Lee did not expect a response. He turned his attention towards Adam before exiting the barn and moving back towards the house. The headmaster met him in the middle of the yard.

"You done with the Negra?"

"Yes, sir. He should be fit for auction in a few days. I did what I could for that leg. I'm afraid it's not gonna be of much use."

"If he can follow a mule, that will be good enough. You haven't heard or happen to have seen a group of Negra boys? We had about eight ready for sale and that one in there cut 'em loose. I can't get top dollar for him, so I'd like to find the others or this trip will be a bust."

"We don't get a lot of traffic this way. From what I hear, most of the sympathizers live on the other side of the river, up near the border. Sheriff and his boys patrol the banks looking for runaways. Every now and then, they'll bring me a woman with child or one that's septic from a miscarriage. Other than that, I try to stay clear. My wife and I take care of each other and try to keep the townsfolk up and going, ain't much room for nothing else. You married?"

The headmaster laughed. "My first wife died of smallpox. Second one died moving out this way from up north. Ain't met another willing to put up with me. I'm too old a dog to chase. I spend my time hunting Negras and running the auctions. Keeps me and my boys moving. Better that way."

"A gypsy's spirit. Good man. I've watered the horses, brushed them down, and given them a good feeding. They should not give you any trouble the rest of the way."

"Thank you, Doc. I'm grateful to you and the Mrs. for the victuals and the hospitality. Nothing like hot food and a stiff drink to make a man feel like himself. I'll get my men together, and we'll be on our way. If you should happen to hear anything about dem Negra boys, I'd appreciate your sending word to the auctioneer. We'll be in town a few days before heading back to Charleston. Might even be a reward in it if we catch 'em."

The headmaster gave Lee a firm slap on the shoulder before turning to walk towards the house.

"I'll definitely keep that in mind."

Lee turned towards the barn. He looked up at the loft and saw Matthew's tiny face staring back at him. He gave a small nod and turned to trace the headmaster's footsteps to the house.

Matthew watched the men walk away. He moved away from the window and quickly descended the ladder to where Adam lay sleeping. He knelt next to him and touched his sleeping frame. Matthew reached around his neck and removed the seashell his father had given him. He gently lifted Adam's head and pulled the twine over it, touching the amulet with his fingers.

"*Amani* [peace] *na Ulinzi* [protection], *Kaka*."

Matthew placed his arms around Adam's sleeping frame and squeezed. He said a silent prayer before releasing him and moving away. He heard Lee and the *bwana* coming towards the barn. He made his way out of the stall and quickly up the ladder back into the shadows of the loft. He watched as one of the *bwana* pulled Adam off the ground, bound his wrist and feet before tossing him onto the back of the mule. The *bwana* mounted their horses and rode away. A few moments later, Lee and Elizabeth entered the barn.

"It's okay to come down, son."

Matthew hesitated before leaving the safety of the loft. He peeked over the edge down at Lee before moving towards the ladder. He descended slowly and walked towards the couple. Elizabeth watched him pensively. Matthew stopped in front of them.

"Thank you for helping my brother."

Matthew resumed his trek towards the house. Lee and Elizabeth stared after him. Lee reached for his wife's hand. Pulling her close, he whispered softly, "We have to be careful. I don't trust that man. We'll have to wait to move the boys in case he's left a scout. I'll check the perimeter in a few days to be certain they're gone. Send word to Donovan and the others that we'll be late pushing the boys through. Things are going to get more complicated now that we're on the radar. I suspect the headmaster will alert the Sheriff, so we may get some unexpected visitors for a while."

Elizabeth looked at her husband with alarm.

"Don't worry, dear. It will be fine. We'll make some adjustments with the others, but nothing stops. We'll keep the roads open. Anyone who comes here will be safe."

Lee kissed his wife and held her close. "God's watching over us and these boys. They'll make it."

*****

Joseph
Kisumu, Kenya

Joseph sat in the rear of the room watching his classmates struggle with the assignment on the blackboard. It was an advanced trig problem. Joseph scrawled out the steps and waited to see if his colleagues would find the errant cosine the teacher had deliberately embedded in the logic. The two stared at the board and moved from side to side, erasing one section, reapplying the numbers and erasing another. Finally, the instructor called time. The previous students sat down as two more approached the board.

Joseph watched this go on for another five minutes before he and his partner were called to the board. Joseph immediately went to the middle of the problem and removed the cosine replacing it with the specific formula necessary to pull the problem into focus. As soon as he completed the script, his partner wrote out the last of the calculation and both returned to their seat.

The instructor continued with class and gave each of the students their assignments for the week. As the students filtered out into the midday sun, she called Joseph to her desk.

"Have you given any thought to my suggestion that you go to the States for the summer? I'd like to discuss the option with your parents but not unless you agree that it is something you'd like to experience. It is an excellent opportunity that may produce some additional scholarships for any future endeavors you have towards college."

"I have given it considerable thought. I am intrigued by the idea…" Joseph stopped his thoughts. He knew his father would not agree to the proposal. The idea that his eldest son would consider leaving to go anywhere outside the confines of their homestead was blasphemous.

The instructor looked at Joseph and smiled.

"Your mother and I met a few days ago in the market. I mentioned the internship and she was very excited. She is in favor of the idea."

Joseph was not surprised. His mother believed her children deserved every opportunity regardless of its origin. He knew from discussions with his aunt that his mother was in her third year at university when she'd met his father. When she'd become pregnant with Joseph, she'd left school and moved to the village to marry. Joseph often saw her sitting in the garden reading her old textbooks or looking through the various magazines at the market. He'd given her a collection of art books he'd won at school for her birthday. At night, after putting his siblings to bed, she'd flip through the pages, touching each, smiling at some unknown thought. Joseph often wondered what she would have become had she not married his father.

"I can have Principal Okuwa speak on your behalf. The deadline for submitting candidates is tomorrow. I have an application ready for you, Joseph, but I need your parents' consent. Talk to your father."

"Yes, ma'am."

Joseph left the classroom and started the four-mile journey home. The sun was hot and the dust from the fields circled his path in wispy tornadoes as he strolled along the river. He'd read about the psychological studies taking place in New York. He had copies of some of the transcripts. He'd listened to several of the lectures and had seen a few of the online presentations. Everything he'd comprehended solidified his desire to study psychology. He'd been writing in his journal for years and each time he reread an entry, somewhere in the subtext were the analogies he'd always seen and the link he knew existed across the ocean. The place where he'd find the answer to the voices in his head and the stories he could never quite finish.

As he rounded the corner of the village, he saw his father at the blacksmith's shop turning the base of the horseshoe he'd molded for the army's fleet. He approached quietly and placed his books and notes in the small locker his father had created for his thirteenth birthday. The wooden box was weathered and blackened with soot, but Joseph loved the feel of the grain against his palm each time he touched it.

He pushed his head through the top of his smelting apron and joined his father next to the anvil. As if the heat from the sun was not stifling enough, the smoke and arid fumes from the fire served to intensify the inferno.

"Hello, Father," Joseph yelled over the ping of his father's hammering.

"Good day, Mwana. How were your classes?"

"We've moved into calculus. I like the logic."

"Very good. The country needs engineers and architects. These skills will serve you well."

Joseph winced at the reference.

"Father, may we talk for a moment?"

Joseph's father looked up from his work with the hammer in midair. "Are you well?"

"Yes, Father. I want to talk about school."

"Are you having troubles in your studies?"

"No. No, Father. Everything is fine. I want to talk about where I wish to go for my advanced studies."

"We can discuss that tonight with your mother. We must complete this order before the General arrives. I promised him an entire set. Let us work and talk later."

Joseph stood still while his Father continued to smelt. After a moment, he took the hammer and began beating the medal furiously.

"Good, Mwana. I will forge the remaining molds and bring them."

Joseph did not see his father walk away nor had he heard what his father had said. His mind channeled his anger into the head of the hammer as he smelted the medal against the anvil. In his head, he was formulating the words he'd say to his parents to convince them he should go to New York. In reality, he was putting his plans in place to leave as soon as he heard from the committee.

As the embers burned around his feet, he watched them smolder and die realizing that if he did not leave, he'd meet the same fate.

*****

Joseph sat beside his sister, Izzy, at the dinner table. He and his father had completed the order of horseshoes and had arrived home just before dark. Joseph had gone straight to his room after listening to his father lament over not being paid for the work. This was a normal occurrence when dealing with the Generals. The rebels ran the country side. If you did not do business with them, you did not do business.

Joseph's father was an asset. His skills as a blacksmith were useful so he and his family were afforded an existence without much distress. The same could not be said for many of Joseph's classmates. The majority of the girls had been bartered off to the rebel forces to ensure their families were not pushed off their homesteads. Many of Joseph's peers were among the soldiers that periodically raided the villages, pillaging what little the people managed to salvage from their gardens and occupations.

Every day, Joseph walked past the mass graves where his grandparents were buried. He passed the dilapidated cabins and the massive fields left to rot because the rebels did not allow anyone across the borders to farm.

The longer Joseph stayed, the more desperate he felt. Ever since the night he'd been tossed into the tunnel with his siblings, he'd sworn to do everything he could to obliterate the tribal traditions that fostered the chaos around him.

"Mwana! Wake up, boy. Your mother is speaking to you."

Joseph saw his Father's lips moving before he heard the words. He turned towards his mother and smiled.

"Yes, Mother. I am sorry. I was lost in my thoughts."

Joseph's mother smiled at him from the opposite end of the table. "Mrs. Patel speaks of a program in the States. She'd like for you to apply. Have you discussed it with your Father?"

Joseph turned from his mother to his father and watched as the man shoveled pieces of stewed lamb into his mouth. Father looked up from the bowl and stopped chewing as if he was unsure of what to say.

"Joseph's place is here. He has siblings. He is to take over the shop. What can he accomplish in the States that he cannot do here?"

Joseph put his fork down and cleared his thoughts. His mother had deliberately broached the subject, and now he had no choice but to fight for what he wanted.

"Father. I am not leaving for good. I am going to study; to experience something unique so that I can come back and make things different."

Joseph's father stared at him over the bowl of soup before rising and moving away from the table, an indication that the subject would not be discussed in the presence of his brother and sisters. Joseph's mother got up and followed her husband into the outer room. As Joseph rose, Izzy grabbed his hand and gave it a gentle squeeze. He knew she was depending on him to build the bridge for her and the others to have the opportunity when the time came. Joseph smiled down at his little sister and bent to give her a kiss before moving away from the table.

When he entered the room, Father was seated in his favorite chair. Mother was perched next to him on the couch. Joseph stopped in the doorway; balanced between where he was and his bid towards his future.

"Mother has explained that she is in favor of your leaving."

Joseph watched Father turn to his wife and place his hand gently on her knee before turning back to his son.

"Explain why?"

Father sat back in the seat with his arms folded across his chest, defiant and stoic. Joseph swallowed hard before opening his mouth. When he did, he prayed for the right words.

"Every day, the rebels come to take someone away. Every day I look to see who has not returned. You and Mother gave up your lives to move the four of us away from the soldiers. I remember the night you pushed us into the tunnel. I thought I would never see you again. I made a promise to Izzy and Thomas that I would be there for them, that I would protect them and that I would make life better for them."

"How is leaving going to make life better? How can you protect your sisters from a country an ocean away? What is to become of my business? Your mother? Have you not considered any of this in your selfish need to run away?"

Father rose from the chair and walked over to his son.

"When I met your mother, she was a beautiful girl on a college campus. I was a young fool from the outskirts of the villages. Your grandfather had been killed in the wars. Uncle had raised me to be a blacksmith and that was all I knew. Do you think I wanted to live on the street? Do you think I enjoyed being homeless and constantly trying to avoid being shot, or worse, having to shoot someone else?

"I married your mother because of you. I built a life for us because of you. I do what I do every day because of you and your siblings. Now you want to leave. For what? A dream of returning to make things better? There is no better, Mwana. There is nothing beyond what you see when you walk out that door. I sacrifice every day to keep this family safe. To keep your mother and sisters out of the camps and you and your brother away from the expeditions. Why should I condone your leaving? Why should I allow you to run away from something I did not?"

Joseph's father stood in front of him with his hands by his side. He was a big man and Joseph had always seen him as supernatural and capable of anything. But at this very moment, Joseph felt cornered and angry. He realized his path to what lay in his future was on the other side of his father's wishes. He grounded himself and steadied his thoughts. When he spoke, he felt calm and confident, unafraid and sure of what he'd decided to do.

"You cannot stop me, Father. My life is here, but my journey to finding my place, my destiny is not. I am thankful for all that you've done. I am grateful to you for giving me life, but in order to live it, I must leave." Joseph hesitated before reaching down and taking his father's hands in his own. "I am not a blacksmith, Father. I am your Mwana. I would rather leave with your blessing than go without it, but the outcome will not change."

Joseph's father stared at his son for a long moment. He squeezed Joseph's hands, released them and returned to his wife's side. He placed a gentle kiss on her forehead, gathered his spear and cloak, and left without a word. Joseph moved to follow.

"No! Let him go." Joseph's mother stood and walked towards her son. "He will return. Come. Finish dinner and talk with your siblings. This may be the last time for a long while that you'll have the opportunity to do so face to face."

*****

Queens, New York

Joseph stepped off the plane at LaGuardia Airport. He heaved his book bag over his shoulders and tugged his suitcase behind him. He retrieved the address from his pocket along with the name of the individual he was scheduled to meet: Professor VanMore. He smiled. It sounded like something from an Alfred Hitchcock movie.

He moved his way through the crowd of individuals surging towards baggage claim, following the rotating Exit signs. Children with arms folded around teddy bears, parents with looks of angst after a long flight with a tired baby, lovers holding hands strolling along the walkway oblivious to everything but their private euphoria. Joseph took it all in as he rounded each corner. He felt relieved yet anxious. He had 800 dollars in his pocket and an international calling card, the sum total of his entire life savings. His suitcase contained two suits, four outfits (including two he'd bought in town waiting for his flight), three pairs of shoes, and all his notes, journals, and books. He was literally starting with nothing, and yet he felt better than he had in years.

Joseph searched the corridors and signs for his meeting point. At the end of the hallway, above a sea of yellow and blue turbans, he saw a giant green banner with bright orange characters that had his last name in crude letters across the front. He smiled and made his way towards the sign. As he approached the gentleman, he smiled at the Colonel Sander's suit and cowboy boots that greeted him.

"Joseph Iglaysia?"

"Yes. Yes, sir."

"Nice to meet you, son. Follow me. We're parked right outside here. Just have to make our way through this cacophony of humanity. How was your flight? No, no. Wait. Let's broach that subject in the sanctity of peace. This way."

Joseph found himself running to keep up with the man. He pulled the suitcase under his arm and trotted down the corridor towards a set of double doors. The two exited the space into a barrage of cars and buses. People were everywhere. The professor led him to a late-model Lincoln town car. He opened the trunk and tossed his bags inside before sliding into the back seat with the professor.

"Troy. Take us to the university."

The car jerked to life and eased into traffic. Soon, they were on the interstate, slowly making their way in and out of the throng of cars.

"Welcome to the US, son. How was your flight?"

"Wonderful. I slept the entire way. I suppose that was nerves or perhaps fear. I think it might have been a combination of both."

"Flying for the first time can be an experience, but we are bound by no other means for occasions that warrant such. Needless to say, we are delighted to have you as a member of the team. In the time I've been affiliated with the program, I've watched students like you develop into magnificent contributors that foster growth and excitement in what is arguably a rather mundane, if not hugely stereotypical, field of study. I am most eager to watch you continue that legacy."

"I appreciate the vote of confidence, Professor."

"I've spoken with Principal Okuwa and Mrs. Patel. They both speak very highly of you. Excellent work ethic. Very bright and intuitive. Progressive. These are traits that will serve you well in your studies."

Joseph was surprised to hear that he'd been the subject of Professor Van More's queries.

"I am flattered that you've taken an interest."

"I take the time to get to know all my interns. I learned a long time ago the best way to keep ahead of the curve is to observe. My time in the classroom and my research have only served to reinforce that philosophy. Experience shapes people. If you come to understand their experiences, you began to understand them."

Joseph was pleased to hear his thoughts echoed in the professor's words.

"How long have you been with the university?"

"I have worked with various colleagues in the field for many years. Most of them have passed through the walls of NYU at some point in their professional destinations. I have called New York my cerebral incubator for several years, but I have only been on staff officially for the past eight years. It has been a glorious ride. My wife and I enjoy the winters."

"I've heard such horror stories, but I am excited to experience the phenomenon for myself."

"You are in for a treat. We will revisit your enthusiasm after a few months in the thick of it."

The two shared a laugh. The Global Center for Academic and Spiritual Life creased the skyline. Joseph watched from the window as the car moved through the throng of students and faculty. It was difficult to tell where the city stopped and the campus began, with the exception of the purple and white NYU banners flapping in the wind. Students huddled on corners shifting book bags from shoulder to shoulder, conversing in exaggerated gesticulations.

The car stopped. The driver exited and retrieved Joseph's bags. He shook the professor's hand and returned to the vehicle. The car disappeared in the sea of people as Joseph and the professor moved passed the patrons on the walk into the building.

The sun filtered through the windows casting beautiful shades of light throughout the corridor. The building hummed with activity as people exited elevators and moved through the lobby. Joseph followed the professor down a hallway and around an enclosure to a waiting room.

"I'll let you take a moment to collect your thoughts and make any contacts while I get your room and schedule confirmed. If all has gone as planned, it will be a simple matter of picking up your key and badge. If the bureaucrats have made a home, it may take a tad longer. Let us pray for a government shut down."

The professor smiled at his euphemism and disappeared into the building. Joseph took off his backpack and placed it and his suitcase against the wall. He pulled out the calling card he'd purchased at the airport and dialed his uncle's number. His mother picked up on the fourth ring.

"Hello? Joseph? Is that you? Have you made it? Are you alright?"

"Mama. Hello. Yes. I am fine. The flight was wonderful. The professor is very nice. I am here, Mama."

"Wonderful, Mwana. Have you eaten?"

Joseph laughed.

"No, Mama. I just arrived. The professor is locating my paperwork. I will call when I have settled into my room. I love you, Mama. I love you all."

*****

New York, New York

Joseph sat in Professor Van More's outer office reading over his final. He'd passed with a B, but he was not happy with the grade. The two questions he'd missed were analogous, first-year prep. Joseph had written a small dissertation for each and suspected his instructor had not even bothered to read the response and had merely marked them incorrect. The thought bothered him more than it probably should have, but he was extra sensitive to his status on campus and was eager to prove that he belonged.

"Joseph. Hello, my boy. Come in, please."

"Good afternoon, professor. You requested my presence?"

"A year and a half, and you're still as formal as the day we met. I am amused by that each time we have occasion to speak. Yes. I have an assignment for you, or rather, an opportunity. If I understand correctly, you're making strides to formulate independent study sessions with the psychology labs in Accra."

"Yes, sir."

"In my short tenure at Berkley, I wrote a diminutive thesis on sleep neurology. At the time, there was no funding for any additional research, so I moved on.

"My grant writing team has come across some interesting chatter about a developing field that could warrant revisiting this particular chain of thought. I believe you've committed to pursuing your Masters, and I'd like to fund that effort if you agree to work with my team to develop the outline for this new endeavor.

"I'd lead the venture myself but am currently unable to devote any additional time to this particular project in conjunction with my various levels of responsibility."

Joseph saw a shadow crease the professor's brow. He'd heard from some of the professor's colleagues that his wife was ill and that her care required most of the professor's time and energies.

"I'm honored you'd choose me, professor, but there have to be other students worthy of the opportunity."

"I have a list of individuals I could present to the board but none rank above you in work ethic or tenacity. The university trusts my judgment, and I believe having you at the helm will ensure the funding is sound and that the core of the project is relevant. Let the naysayers take issue with me if there is anything to be disputed."

"But I am a junior researcher. There are residents and interim professors that should be considered."

Professor VanMore pulled out a chair next to Joseph and sat down. He stared at Joseph for a moment before he spoke.

"Are you afraid of failure, Joseph?"

"No, sir."

"Do you believe you are incapable of doing what I have asked?"

"No, sir."

"Do you feel the knowledge, support, and network you build here will aid your goals when you return home?"

"Yes, sir."

"Then why do you continue to formulate theories in direct conflict to the outcome you seek?"

Joseph did not respond.

"As the Dean of Studies, my word is law. I am not an autocrat in that I feel the need to pull rank; however, I have made it perfectly clear to any who have an interest that you are to facilitate the logic upon which this particular level of research will advance. The only hindrance would be your refusal."

Joseph was dumbfounded. "I don't know what to say, professor."

"That would be a first." Professor VanMore smiled and stood up. He walked over to his desk and retrieved a large folder.

"Here are the preliminary specs based on notes from my initial thesis. It contains all the data you need to formulate the case studies and put together a team. I will be closely involved with each stage of the project, but any and all decisions concerning the foundation will come directly from you. Do you have any questions?"

"No, sir."

"Excellent."

Professor VanMore reached to shake Joseph's hand and pulled him up from the chair before rushing him towards the office door.

"I am expecting a potential donor in about fifteen minutes and am ashamed to say that I am not nearly as prepared as I should be to make her acquaintance. I will give you a few days to come to terms with the assignment. It is always a pleasure to work with you, Joseph. I believe this is merely another stone in our mutual journey. Take care, son. Talk to you soon."

Joseph heard the door close behind him as he moved down the hallway. He felt the weight of the folder in his hand as his feet continued to move. When he exited the building, he made his way to a bench a few feet away and sat down. He felt winded.

"What just happened?"

He opened the folder and saw a bright red envelope on top. He picked it up and opened it. Inside, he found a neat one-page letter.

>Dearest Joseph,
>
>I reasoned you'd have a hard time accepting my proposal.
>
>I've spoken to several of your professors, and they all agree that you're not working to your peak aptitude. I realize you're a long way from home and some would say that is a mitigating factor, but I do not believe that is the case. You underestimate your talents.
>
>I apologize that I am unable to provide the support you may require. Unfortunately, my personal obligations have become a necessity I did not anticipate. However, I am confident that this endeavor will push you to realize what I already know.
>
>I am more than confident that you'll live up to my expectations and exceed your own.

Joseph folded the letter and placed it back in the envelope. He got up from the bench and turned towards his dorm. He had a tremendous amount of work ahead but first he intended to visit his psychology professor to discuss his final.

*****

Manhattan, New York

"Jackie."

"Yes, my love."

Professor VanMore sat on the edge of the bed with his eyes closed. He'd been up all night with Miriam trying to coax her with liquids to prevent dehydration. She was in excellent spirits albeit weak and in pain.

"You know what I'd like?" Miriam's voice was hoarse and barely above a whisper; her breathing labored.

"Tell me and it is yours."

"Do you remember those brownies we had in Paris? The ones with the crème da la cream on top. They were delicious."

Professor VanMore smiled. "Delivery may take a while, but I will see what I can do."

The professor rose from the edge of the bed and walked around to his wife's side. Her gaunt frame looked pale against the cotton sheets. Jackson pulled the comforter up over her shoulder and knelt beside her.

"I'm tired, Jackie."

"I know, my love. Rest. It will help."

"You're missing your classes. I'm keeping you from your work, your students."

"None of that matters. Nothing is more important to me than being here discussing Parisian brownies with you."

Miriam smiled, and Jackson felt his heart sink. He kissed his wife and held her hand. The cold appendage felt light against his palm. He squeezed it gently and felt Miriam respond with a weak pat against his fingers. She opened her eyes and smiled at him again.

"You need to go out."

"It's raining. Traffic's atrocious. I'm safer here then out with the villains that litter the highways with potholes and trash. Life is much easier within these walls."

Miriam raised her hand and stroked her husband's sideburns.

"Time for a trim."

Jackson burst into laughter. He kissed his wife's hand.

"Sleep, cherie."

He sat next to her until her breathing slowed into an uneven pattern. Easing from the bed, he moved around the room quietly before exiting into the den. He picked up the phone and dialed the international operator before placing the call to his eldest son in Germany.

"Hello, Andrew."

"Dad? It's 2:00 a.m."

"Call your brother. The two of you need to come to see your mother."

There was silence on the other end.

"The chemo is not going well. The doctors say its spread to her lungs. They are not optimistic the new treatment's going to work."

"They aren't even willing to try?"

"Your mother's not willing to try. She's tired and in pain. She doesn't want this. I don't want this for her."

"But, Dad—"

"Andrew. I'm not giving up, son. I'm letting go."

Jackson heard his son sigh on the other end.

"I'll call Darius. We'll be on the first flight as soon as we can make arrangements. I'll send the itinerary when it's complete."

"Thank you, Drew."

Jackson hung up the phone and listened to the house settle. He closed his eyes, took a couple of deep breaths and dialed the number in Oklahoma.

"Hello. Dad? Everything okay?"

"Hey, baby. You and Michael need to make arrangements to come and see your mother."

"Daddy. No. Please."

"I know, baby. This is not easy for me either. The doctors have done all they can. They want me to move her to hospice but that's not an option. I'm making arrangements to have a nurse come here."

"There's nothing they can do? Nothing? I thought we agreed to try the experimental—"

"Angela. Baby. Your mother's as stubborn as you are. She won't."

Jackson felt his daughter's sobs on the other side of the receiver.

"Hey, Pop," Angela's husband quipped from the other end. "We'll leave first thing. We'll be there as soon as we can."

"I appreciate that, son. Thank you."

The phone went dead. Jackson felt numb. His mind wouldn't function. The room felt cold and empty. He reached for the cup of water he'd retrieved from the kitchen and felt his fingers lose grip. He watched the cup hit the floor. The water cascaded across the hardwood floor beneath the armchair. Jackson did not move. He closed his eyes and felt the sting from his repressed tears burn. He pushed his face into his hands and silently wept into the darkness.

*****

New York, New York

Knock. Knock.

Joseph stood outside Professor VanMore's office. He'd compiled his notes and was ready to give an overview of the project's progress in response to the Professor's request.

"Come in."

Joseph entered the office quickly. He was on edge without actually knowing why. He'd prepared for this recitation for months. There was nothing he couldn't answer, yet he felt an underlying sense of anxiety. As he moved across the floor, he noticed the office was dimly lit. Most of the illumination came from the large windows that lined the walls of the professor's office. Professor VanMore's back was to him.

"Have a seat, Joseph. I'll be right with you."

Joseph took a seat in one of the large armchairs. The professor's office, though sparsely decorated, was furnished like a comfortable sitting room. Joseph flipped through his notes while the professor completed his call.

"Yes. I understand. Please be reminded that this is a charitable affair. Yes. Yes. Again, I understand, but what I am attempting to relay, to avoid any ambiguity, is that the majority of the expenses to host the affair have already been mitigated. There is nothing required but the space. We have a caterer. Yes. We have servers. There will be security. Again, nothing is required from your staff but opening the building and closing the facility once the event is complete. All other areas of concern have been covered by my staff. Yes, I understand that the price includes the aforementioned services. We are very pleased that you are willing to decrease the overall cost by removing such, but it is not necessary. As I have stated, payment has been funded and is available."

Joseph heard the professor take a deep breath and let it out slowly, signifying that he was irritated by the individual on the other end and the overall tone of the call.

"Mr. Gronbowski, if I could have a moment to complete a sentence. Thank you. I appreciate your taking the time to call. Rest assured your conscientiousness will be taken into account for any future events we choose to host. The terms of the contract are sound; payment is available for remittance at the behest of your agency as soon as the proper routing information is relayed or via credit card if such is required. We have paid the retainer, secured the facility, and my people are in place. There is no need for additional deliberation. I am a busy man, and the time I have allocated to this endeavor, albeit gracious on your part, has been wholly unnecessary, as your staff was more than efficient in their handling of my request. The event is a month away, all is in place, and for all intents and purposes, there is no need for any additional input. I appreciate your taking the time to call, but I really must end this conversation. Good-bye."

The professor hung up the phone and turned away from the windows to face his office. Joseph had not seen the man in three months. During his wife's illness, the professor had taken a short leave from his duties. He and Joseph had brief conversations over the phone or via email but today was the first face-to-face. The professor looked worn. He'd lost weight, and the characteristic laugh lines around his cheeks and eyes appeared to droop and sag in on themselves. Normally very meticulous about his appearance, he wore a jacket over a plain turtleneck sweater with a pair of denim slacks.

He placed the phone on his desk, ran his hand across his face, and sat silently before raising his eyes towards Joseph.

"My apologies, my boy. My family and I are hosting a charity event at one of the local venues. We're expecting upwards of 10,000 individuals. The location boasts the capacity, but in dealing with the event manager, it has been a nightmare to coordinate. They are insistent that we utilize their staff when the young lady with whom I signed the contract was very clear that it was not a requirement. I've spent the last two days attempting to convince the man that my only requirement is the facility. Apparently, he is having a difficult time accepting the terms. I was hoping to circumvent having my daughter engage the situation, but it appears that may be necessary." The professor smiled. "Needless to say, the situation will be handled by the end of the day. Now, let us move on to the subject at hand."

The professor opened a file on his desk. Joseph assumed it was the report he'd submitted. The one he had a copy of in his file and had written from the notes he'd been perusing since entering the office.

"I'm glad to see that the team has secured four of the six grants the research crew provided. That will more than facilitate the space and resources we need to set up a lab and fund the necessary equipment."

Professor VanMore continued to read.

"It also shows here that you've engaged the assistance of three interns from the sister school in New Jersey. Any particular reason you chose these three students over ones here? Though interns, we will have to expend a stipend to facilitate their travel. Is that necessary?"

"The individuals in question are transfers that will be moving their current credits to NYU. I engaged their expertise based on essays and surveys we posted to vet potential interns. These particular students provided feedback in line with theories purported in your initial thesis: chronotherapy, circadian rhythms, and parasomnias. Of the fifty essays screened, these students appear to be viable candidates for team leads that can structure the test cases. The final nod will be based on your assessment, but I reasoned it beneficial to secure their services before they were otherwise engaged."

The professor smiled. "You never cease to amaze me, Joseph. It's as if you've lived inside my head. I agree with your hypothesis. My apologies for questioning your decision."

The professor continued to study the folder. He asked Joseph a few more questions before shifting the tone of the conversation. He closed the folder and gazed at Joseph for a moment before speaking.

"How is your family?"

Joseph sat a moment, uncertain how to answer.

"Mother and Father are well. My oldest sister is preparing for university. During my last visit, I petitioned to have my two younger siblings' studies moved to a location closer to my parent's homestead. I am pleased to report that it has been granted. The move will take considerable worry from my mother, for that I am most thankful."

"And how are you? I have been rather neglectful of my duties as emissary. I fear several of my shining stars may be suffering from my lack of engagement."

Joseph felt empathy for the professor's plight. He'd taken it upon himself to nurture his interns and was punishing himself for the supposed failure. Joseph appreciated the gesture even though it was totally unwarranted.

"I am doing well, professor. And from what I can assess, the other interns are doing so also. We have taken it upon ourselves to be self-sufficient during your brief sabbatical."

The professor smiled. "Excellent. Spring break is approaching. Do you have plans to return home?"

"No, sir. In light of my recent visit, I chose to accompany my roommate to his hometown of Charleston. He articulates such animated tales of the city, I am intrigued to witness the colloquialisms up close and personal. Not to mention, sample the local cuisine. He speaks of the Gullah with reverence. I have researched the group and find many of their traditions mirror rituals from home. I am also interested to engage in some of the particulars."

"You plan to accomplish quite a lot in a week. You are in for a treat. Nothing like submerging yourself in the familiar only to discover that it is not quite such."

The two chatted amiably for a while until Joseph's cell phone pinged denoting an alert for another meeting.

"Always a pleasure, my boy. I appreciate your taking the time to entertain an old man's whims. I am pleased with your progress. You have done an admirable job. I look forward to the next few months as we continue to fine tune the team and the preliminary stages of the study. I'll await your next updates while I continue to digest your most recent acquisitions and thoughts. Enjoy your time in Charleston. I look forward to hearing about your adventures and your observations."

*****

Charleston, South Carolina

Joseph sat in the rocking chair across from his roommate's parents with a plate of food in his lap; smothered chicken, sweet potatoes, red rice, turnip greens, and a hunk of corn bread the size of a loaf of bread. On the table next to him sat a bowl of blueberry cobbler and a large Arnold Palmer. He assessed the meal, uncertain where to start.

"Is everything okay, Joseph?" Mrs. Sorenson inquired.

"Yes, ma'am. Everything's fine. I'm just not certain what I want to try first."

The woman smiled, pleased to have the opportunity to dazzle her son's friend with her culinary talents.

"Don't you worry. There's plenty. You eat as much as you want."

Joseph watched his roommate, Keyth, and Mr. Sorenson tear into the food like they'd not eaten in weeks. He took a forkful of potatoes and pushed them forward. The creamy goodness filled his mouth with joy as he scooped up a forkful of greens, followed by a rectangular chunk of the cornbread. He smiled at Mrs. Sorenson as he pushed red rice into the gravy and shoveled the mixture behind the greens. Everything was delicious, and before he'd realized it, Joseph was running a wedge of bread around the edges of the plate to capture the last remnants of the gravy. He dropped his fork on his plate and sat back, appraising the blueberry cobbler. His mind rejected the signals from his stomach. As much as he wanted to try the dessert, it would have to wait.

Joseph noticed a soft ringing in his ears. He turned towards the yard to assess if there was anything present that would account for the sudden advent of the noise, but nothing caught his attention. He turned back towards the house and instead of the vaulted windows and cream-colored tile, Joseph saw darkness.

Adam
Charleston, South Carolina

Adam rolled the bushel of grain onto the back of the wagon before hoisting himself up to tie it in place. He eased his bad leg around the side and bent down to secure the grain to the rafters before standing up.

He'd deliberately parked the wagon across the road so he'd have to walk from the store, down the street, and crossways the courtyard. He needed to exercise his left leg. It had been almost two years since he'd been sold to a plantation on the outskirts of town. It had taken six months for his leg to heal, and even now, it stiffened up when he wasn't active. He could put weight on it and walk, but he still couldn't run.

He jumped up on the wagon and rapped the reigns across Jethro's back. The animal neighed in protest before jerking forward. Moving along the road, Adam hummed to himself. He rarely talked to anyone on the plantation so the trips to town afforded him the opportunity to vent his vocal chords. Down the road, he saw an approaching wagon. He steered the horse to the far side and slowed the pace.

Coming towards him was a white woman and a female slave. The two were talking animatedly, laughing even. Adam cautiously kept his eyes on the road, but he stole a glance at the pretty, dark-skinned girl steering the horses. She smiled in his direction as the two passed, and Adam felt his heart flutter. He waited until he was a good way down the road before turning to watch the wagon retreat.

He'd seen his auntie in that smile. The realization saddened him, but the thought of seeing it again filled him with a joy he hadn't felt since he'd lost her and his brothers. Hope was something he'd forgotten existed, but he'd caught a glimpse of it and he was eager to find a way to experience it face to face the first opportunity he was given.

*****

Adam walked into the general store with his head bowed and his eyes low. He'd been sent to town to pick up several pieces of material for the mistress of the house and some smaller items for her cook, Aunt Betty. He walked up to the counter and handed Mr. Taftin the note he'd been given.

"Good morning, Adam."

"Good morning, sir," Adam returned in an even tone.

"No need for the wagon today I see."

"No, sir."

Adam moved to the far end of the store and kept his eyes low to avoid making eye contact with the women moving around the counter. He'd seen several of his colleagues severely beaten for imaginary winks at the female patrons. Mr. Taftin noted the stance and continued servicing the ladies until he'd helped each one and emptied the store.

"Adam. It's okay for you to come over to the counter. There's no one here."

Adam reluctantly raised his eyes to confirm Mr. Taftin's statement. He slowly lifted his head and cautiously walked over to the counter.

"Mrs. Bannon wants some yellow and blue material today. I've also got that green thread she wanted the last time you were here. No charge for that."

Mr. Taftin moved behind the counter as Adam walked up and down the aisle's looking at the various items on the shelf. He dared not touch anything for fear of being seen, so he kept his hands in his pockets to avoid the urge to pick something up.

He stopped in front of one shelf that contained a small clay figurine. It was an elephant with a beautiful blanket draped over its back. Adam had never seen such a beautiful display. He looked at the piece, raised up on his tiptoes to see if anyone was around. Slowly, he eased his hand out of his pocket and picked up the small piece and held it in his hands. It was light and felt like glass. He rolled it around in his fingers, marveling at the multicolored animal. He quickly put the piece back in place and returned to the counter.

"Here you go, Adam. I put Mrs. Bannon's material in this box and Auntie Betty's cooking supplies are in this burlap bag you can put on your back."

Adam took the bag and pulled it over his shoulders. He tucked the box under his arm and locked it against his thigh.

"Do you like the figurine?"

Adam stood very still and did not say a word.

"There's no need to be afraid, Adam," Mr. Taftin assured in a soft tone. "There was a gentleman in last month that bought all the pieces but that one. I'll make you an offer. The next time you come to town, you can do some chores for me around here. Take a couple of items to some of my elderly patrons that don't make it to town that often. When you earn enough, I'll give it to you."

Adam was cautious.

"Think about it, and we'll talk more the next time you come to town."

"Yes, sir."

Adam turned and quickly exited the store. He walked along the street towards the stable. As he sauntered around the tavern, he spotted a wagon on the opposite side of the street. He stopped and waited. He'd seen the wagon before, and he was eager to see if the girl with the pretty smile was driving.

Adam saw her emerge from the bakery with several baskets. She placed them on the wagon before going back into the bakery. He walked across the street towards the entrance. The smell of fresh baked bread and confections filled his nostrils as he made his way into the space. He stopped in front of a rack of rolls and felt his mouth began to water. He saw the young lady coming towards him with several large baskets.

"Afternoon, sis. If you'd like, I can help with those?"

"You appear to have an armful already."

Adam felt the elegant tempo of her words reach his eardrums. He shifted the box to the front of his body and hoisted it out towards her.

"It's not heavy. You can place the baskets on top. I can carry them out for ya."

The young lady smiled and placed the two large baskets on top of the box in Adam's arms.

"If you drop those, I'll have your hide."

She rotated to return to the bakery counter while Adam made his way out to the wagon. He balanced the box, walking slowly towards the back. He sat the box down and placed the baskets next to the others. He jumped up into the wagon and found a small piece of rope. Running the rope through each of the basket handles, he secured them to the back of the wagon to ensure they did not slide as the vehicle moved along the road. When he looked up from his task, the young lady was standing there with three more baskets. She placed them on the wagon and hopped up to join Adam.

"These are the last of them."

She gave the baskets to Adam and watched as he secured them to the others. He pulled the knot tight and stepped back to allow her to inspect his work.

"I was thinking about how I was going to make it back to the house without tossing everything out of the baskets and into the back of the wagon. That's pretty clever."

She smiled, and Adam returned one of his own.

"What's your name?"

"Adam."

"Nice to meet you, Adam. My name's Cicely."

"Nice to meet ya, Ms. Cicely."

Cicely smiled at the formality of the salutation.

"Did you walk into town?"

"No, ma'am. My horse is in the stable."

"How far do you live from town?"

"On the other side of the creek north of here."

"You're one of Reynold's."

"Yes'm." Adam kept his voice low and neutral.

Cicely considered her options. She wanted to return Adam's kindness, but Scillia had warned her to stay clear of Reynold's land and his men. They were known for night raids and any Negra caught on their side of the Mason-Dixon was considered Reynold's property by right of trespassing.

"I can take you as far as my cabin."

"I appreciate it, ma'am."

Adam helped Cicely retrieve and load the last of her wares. He jumped up into the wagon and extended his hand towards her. She smiled and climbed up into the seat next to him. Cicely adjusted her skirt and reached down to retrieve the reins, but Adam gently took them from her hand with a smile.

"I'd be happy to drive, ma'am. Jethro's trot is not as quick as your steeds. I wouldn't want to tucker him out on the way."

Cicely moved to the other side of the seat and allowed Adam to exchange into position with the horses. He gave them a light snap. They jumped into a slow trot pulling the wagon along in an easy lull. Adam pushed the vehicle towards the stables to retrieve Jethro. He tethered the horse to the back of the vehicle and resumed his position at the front next to Cicely.

The two rode along in silence at the outset. Adam felt awkward; his mind searching for the means to start a conversation that would prompt Cicely to speak. After a moment, he cleared his throat and began to sing one of his Auntie's favorite songs.

> I got a robe, you got a robe
> All o' God's chillun got a robe
> When I get to heab'n I'm goin' to put on my robe
> I'm goin' to shout all ovah God's Heab'n
> Heab'n, Heab'n
> Ev'rybody talkin' 'bout heab'n ain't goin' dere
> Heab'n, Heab'n

> I'm goin' to shout all ovah God's Heab'n

To his surprise and extreme joy, Cicely began singing as well. Adam listened to the melodic tempo of her voice which seemed to transform the song from what he remembered. The two talked and laughed the entire trip to Cicely's cabin.

Adam stopped the wagon in front of the tiny house and aided Cicely down from the seat. He helped her unload the baskets before untying Jethro and mounting the horse for the journey back to Reynold's plantation.

"Thank you for your help, Adam."

"Ya welcome, ma'am."

"How often do you go to town?"

"Anytime the mistress or Auntie Betty needs something, Jethro and I make our way. We been traveling this road together since he was a yearling." Adam rubbed the horse's ears gently while patting his neck and hunches.

"The next time you're on your way, come by here. I go to town often. Maybe we can help each other along the way, and give Jethro a little rest."

"I'd be much obliged, Ma'am."

Adam tried to suppress his smile. The air felt light, and it seemed as though the birds were singing louder than usual. He could not contain the elation in his heart as he pulled Jethro's reins. The gesture was a means of distracting his thoughts and not so much an indication that he wanted to leave.

Cicely reached into the basket she was holding and pulled out a small brown roll. She handed it to Adam with a smile.

"It's not much. Next time, I'll have something sweeter for you."

Adam reached down and took the bread in his hand. It was still warm and soft. He bit into the parcel.

"Mmmmmmm. Thank ya, ma'am. Not too many occasions where I get treats like this."

"We will have to change that. Get home safe and don't forget to stop by on your way to town."

"Yes'm."

Adam reluctantly snapped the reins across Jethro's back. The horse moved into a slow trot. Adam took another bite of the roll and waved at Cicely as the horse progressed along the road. He watched her move into the tiny house before turning to face where he was going.

Adam felt a joy he could not contain as he opened his mouth full of bread to sing. He bellowed the notes with a renewed vigor to no one in particular but simply to express what he felt inside. Adam was happy. He'd forgotten what it felt like to feel this kind of emotion. He'd forgotten what it was like to hope life could mean something. He'd discovered a reason to live, to try, and to wake up. He'd found a reason to love, and he'd made up in his mind to hold on to it with everything he had.

*****

Cicely pulled the biscuits from the oven. She placed them on the counter and picked up the small cup of honey and butter she'd melted a few minutes earlier. She drizzled the warm liquid over each biscuit, coating the top with a thick layer while the remainder rolled down the sides. The aroma filled the kitchen and moved throughout the house. Scillia sat at the kitchen table with her ledger. She looked up from her calculations and smiled at Cicely.

"Those smell amazing. I hope that's for dinner tonight."

"I'll put them back in the oven just before serving to make certain they'll be warm on the table."

"Excellent. We want to make a good impression on the general and his men. We need the militia on our side. Cicely, come here a moment. I need to show you something."

Cicely emptied the container, wiped her hands on her apron, and moved towards the table where Scillia was seated.

"Yes, Ma'am."

"Since mother passed away, I've been assessing the state of the property. Father accumulated an immense expanse of land, human capital, and livestock. Naturally, his desire was that James step into his birthright but my brother's interest lay in how much everything was worth rather than continuing Father's legacy. Mother never took an interest, so Father put his trust in me."

Scillia smiled at her personal reflections.

"As a Southern woman, it goes against the very institution of who we are that I should consider you a very dear friend and a part of this family, but tradition be damned.

"I've written you into my will. Should anything happen to me, this document gives you and the others freedom. But, most importantly, it states that you are to receive a portion of the estate."

"Scillia. There's not a white man in Charleston County that's going to abide by that piece of paper. And what about James? He won't allow it."

"The courts are very specific. A will is a legally binding article under the laws of South Carolina. No man, black or white, can dispute the law."

Cicely sat at the end of the table with a furrowed brow, wringing her hands. Scillia took them in hers and smiled.

"Cicely. This estate is all I have left of Daddy. If it is within my power, I refuse to allow it to be overrun by a horde of irresponsible slave owners and land mongers. If I marry and have children, the majority of the estate will be allotted to them, but you will remain as a beneficiary."

Scillia hugged Cicely before rising from the table. "Now. I must prepare for the general. He enjoys looking through Father's collection of rifles and handguns. I have a few new ones I need to clean and put in the cabinet."

Cicely sat at the table, watching Scillia collect her ledgers. She watched the woman depart the space before standing to return to her cooking. She absently moved through the kitchen, her mind focused on Scillia's promise. She knew it was not possible but something about Scillia's insistence made her want to believe.

Whack! Cicely jumped at the sound.

Whack!

She put her oven mitts down and walked to the back door. Looking out over the backyard, she saw Adam standing behind a large oak tree. He smiled at her from the shadows.

Cicely turned off the stove, covered the biscuits and stew pot before easing her way out the backdoor. She met Adam at the foot of the hill. The two shared a kiss and hug before Cicely gave him a mason jar full of stew and a towel with two of the honey biscuits.

"Woman, you're gonna make me as fat as a dinner hog."

"You'll freeze if you don't put some meat on your bones."

"I ain't turning down nothin', you cook." Adam smiled from ear to ear as he took a bite of the biscuit. "I have a surprise for you."

"I need to get back to the house. Scillia's entertaining the general this evening."

"You'll be back before dinner. Come on."

Adam took Cicely's hand and began jogging down the hill towards the back of the plantation. The two traveled through a small patch of tightly knit vines and over a small creek before entering a small meadow full of sunflowers.

Adam led Cicely to the base of a large scarlet maple tree. He'd placed a crude vase of sunflowers on a blanket along with a small brown box. He helped Cicely sit before taking his place next to her. He reached for the small box and handed it to her.

Cicely opened the box and sorted through the leaves and flower petals Adam used to hide the object inside. She pulled the tiny parcel free and smiled.

"It's beautiful, Adam."

Cicely held the elephant figurine in the palm of her hand. She picked it up and turned it around between her fingers marveling at the pretty colors. Adam watched her with bated breath. He'd worked with Mr. Taftin for several months to buy the piece. He'd hidden it in Jethro's stall until the right time to give it to Cicely. She'd mentioned to him that she always remembered the day she and her mother were taken from the orchard. She spoke of the occasion with sadness so Adam wanted to give her something to make her think happier thoughts.

"Do you like it?"

"It is beautiful. I remember the elephants when I was a child. This reminds me of home. How did you get it?"

"I carried parcels to Mr. Taftin's customers. I painted the store, and during the evenings, I'd sweep the entire building. He was sick a few months ago. I helped the missus move him from their bedroom downstairs a few times. He gave it to me when he was better. Said I earned it free and clear."

"Thank you, Adam. I love it."

Cicely leaned towards Adam and placed a soft kiss on his cheek. He smiled at her before leaning in for a deeper kiss. The two moved closer together and eased down on the blanket. Adam caressed the contours of Cicely's back and shoulders before moving his hand underneath her skirt. As he did so, he felt an overwhelming desire and realized, rather awkwardly, he had no idea what he was doing. He pulled away quickly and cleared his throat. He stood up and walked towards the small stream. Cicely rolled up on her knees and followed.

"Adam. Thank you."

Cicely moved close to him and wrapped her arms around his waist. She leaned into his back, resting against his weight. Adam felt her warmth move through his body fueling his confusion. When he spoke, his voice felt strained.

"I thought of you every time I saw it on the shelf."

"I'm not just grateful for the gift, but I am happy that I met you."

Cicely pulled her arms away from Adam's waist and gently turned him around to face her. She smiled at him and resumed her position in front of him. Adam wrapped his arms around Cicely's frame and pulled her close. He kissed her on the forehead like his aunt used to when she'd put them to bed.

"I am happy you met me."

Cicely laughed. She pulled away from Adam's embrace and stared at him. She noted the sadness in his eyes.

"You've told me how you came to be on Reynold's plantation, but you've never talked about your brothers or your auntie. You speak fondly of them yet you've never told me their story."

Adam took Cicely's hand and led her back to the blanket. He helped her sit and settled next to her. He took her hand in his and closed his eyes. She watched him closely. When he opened his eyes, he was in a faraway place.

"I never knew my mama. Auntie said they took her away when I was born. The other women told me she was killed tryin' to escape. I didn't pay it no mind. Auntie raised me. She and Uncle taught me everythin' I know.

"Uncle would take me when he'd go huntin'. We took the trails, and he showed me the different creeks. He and my uncles would draw maps and show me how to move through the woods. I'd leave at night. Go out into the forest to catch rabbits and coons. We had stew every winter and enough to share with the other families. I built a tree house when Matthew was born. When he was bigger, we'd go out at night and sleep in the forest. Sometimes we took Elijah, but mostly me and Matthew."

Adam stopped and wiped his face. Cicely reached out and caressed his cheek.

"I watched Auntie's cabin burn. The women said she went inside and never came out. I didn't have nobody else. I had to find my brothers. I promised Auntie. I used everything Uncle taught me to get them safe. When I wake up in da morning and before I close my eyes to rest, I pray they found *uhuru*. Before I met you, that was all I prayed for."

Adam squeezed Cicely's hand and kissed her palm. She moved close and cuddled him in her embrace. Adam felt less afraid as he eased Cicely down on the blanket. He kissed her neck, burying his face in her scent. They moved together slowly, unsure of what to do next.

Cicely reached out and slowly began unbuttoning Adam's shirt. She placed her hand against his chest and felt his heart beating against her palm.

Adam tugged the straps to her blouse and watched them fall open, revealing the soft curve of her breast. He leaned in and gently kissed one, cupping the soft flesh in his hand. Cicely moaned. Emboldened, Adam pulled the blouse over her head and wrapped his arms around her frame. Cicely shivered against him as the dew from the adjacent stream settled on her skin.

Cicely moved from beneath Adam, stood up, and started to unbutton the layers of her skirt. Adam sat transfixed as her fingers moved along the seams. She let the clothing fall, stepped free, and bent over to remove her undergarment corset. Adam watched her kneel in front of him, reach for his hands, and smile.

"*Upendo* [love]. *Uaminifu* [trust] *na furaha* [joy]."

*****

Adam stood at the top of the hill looking down over the valley. He could see the smokestacks of the slave quarters on Reynold's plantation. The men were returning from the fields, and the women sat in the courtyard pulling thread to repair shirts and torn knee patches.

Adam remembered the days he'd come home to find his auntie making a new shirt for his uncle or a pair of breeches for one of the boys. He'd sit next to her on the ground and watch her fingers move across the fabric. She'd taught him how to sew. He'd help her on the days it rained, knitting the winter caps for the newborns or the shawls for the older mothers. They'd talk about the day and the things his aunt had seen while working in the big house in New Orleans. He loved hearing about the river boats and the cemeteries, the large gravestones and the endless rows of houses. Adam closed his eyes and began to sing.

> Walk together children
> Don' you get weary
> Walk together children
> Don't you get weary
> Oh, talk together children
> Don't you get weary
> There's a great camp meeting in the promised land

Cicely sat at the kitchen table shelling butter beans. She had a boiler of Crowder peas on the stove along with a pot of rice and some stewed lamb. She'd washed and dried the mason jars in preparation for the tomatoes and okra she'd picked from the garden. Today was her busy day, the time she put aside while Scillia was in town to stock the panties and prepare the house for the winter months. She stopped. She heard Adam's voice float across the air from the top of the hill.

Cicely smiled and ran her hand across her belly. She was six months along. The baby rolled around as if responding to his father's singing. Cicely twirled the seashell necklace between her fingers. Adam had given it to her the day she'd told him she was pregnant. It was a gift for his unborn son, an heirloom from Adam to his first-born, just as Adam's uncle had given it to Matthew. Cicely laughed. She'd argued it could easily be a girl. Adam scoffed at the thought.

"My first born will be a *mwana*. He shall be named Abraham to honor my uncle."

Cicely had not argued. The mothers had all but confirmed Adam's prediction, but she enjoyed teasing him. She moved away from the table towards the stove. She stirred the rice, checked the peas, and turned the burner off under the lamb. She rinsed the butter beans under the sink and left them to drain while she peeled the tomatoes. She hummed in tune with Adam's singing. She heard the front door open.

"Cicely!"

"In the kitchen."

Scillia entered the space like a whirlwind.

"Those bastards at the courthouse. I swear I need to take one of Daddy's shotguns and kill them all."

"Sit down, woman. I'll fix you a plate of food. That will calm your nerves."

"I don't have time to eat. The General and his men are on the way. They are coming to look at several of our horses. Say they need to confiscate them for the militia. I need to have Thomas move the mares to the far side of the ranch and take the yearlings to the river. I can't have my best horses run in the ground. We've got a field full of cotton and soy beans to push out to market."

"Thomas is in the fields. He won't be back until dark. I can get Adam to help with the horses."

Scillia stopped and smiled at Cicely. "I believe Adam's been around quite enough these last few months."

Cicely blushed.

"If you can get him here in a hurry, I'll be pleased for his assistance."

"He should be coming down from the hills. I'll have him move the mares and the yearlings when he stops in for dinner."

Scillia walked over to the stove and gave Cicely a huge hug. She stepped back and placed her hand on Cicely's belly. She smiled when the baby kicked.

"I'll be upstairs. If you need anything, call. Tell Adam I said hello and thank you."

Cicely continued to move around the kitchen. She'd finished the last of the tomatoes and the peas just when she heard Adam whistle from the yard. She waddled outside with a basket full of victuals.

"Hello, mister."

Adam met her with a kiss and a hug. He stepped back and bent down to kiss her belly.

"*Hujambo, mwana.*"

Adam helped Cicely sit down on the bench outside the house. He opened the basket and pulled out the jar of stewed lamb. He tore into it with vigor.

"I swear you can cook dirt, and I'd eat it," Adam exclaimed with a mouth full of food.

Cicely smiled.

"Scillia needs you to move the horses to the edge of the homestead. The militia's coming, and she wants the good horses out of sight."

"Anything for the Missus. Can I finish my stew?"

"Yes, sir. I'll pack the rest for when you return. You can share it with the field hands."

"No, ma'am. Ain't no other man getting a taste of your victuals. I won't have no one's feet under yo table but mine and my boy's."

Cicely smiled. Adam helped her rise from the table and move back into the house. He kissed her on the cheek before heading towards the barn to move the horses. Adam walked along the path to the barn slowly. He whistled a familiar tune as he rounded the orchard outside the stables. Moving across the landscape, he saw a glint of light in his peripheral.

Adam did not stop. He kept his gait steady as he entered the barn. He moved towards the horses. Calmly cooing to sooth the beasts, he entered the stalls. He gathered the two mares and three yearlings. He tied them to the outside posts before returning to disperse the males in the empty stalls.

After he'd moved each of the male animals, he jumped on the back of the older female and pushed the animals along the stream towards the far end of the valley. He led the horses into a small cluster of trees. He tied each to a separate sturdy branch before making his way back to the house. He tapped the door gently and waited. Cicely appeared at the screen door with a basket in her hands. She smiled but quickly took account of the change in Adam's demeanor when he did not return the gesture.

"What's wrong? Everything go okay with the horses?"

"Yes'm. You can send Thomas to fetch them in the valley. They are tied up in a small group of trees near the stream."

Cicely sensed something was wrong. "Adam. What is it?"

"Nothing, woman. Go back in the house and finish dinner. I'll come back for the victuals. I need to get back to Reynold's before dark."

Cicely pressed but Adam was insistent. He quickly kissed her on the cheek before turning to walk away. She watched him disappear into the trees at the back of the house; she realized in the opposite direction from the road to Reynold's homestead.

*****

Adam walked through the trees, his mind on the gleam of light he'd seen on his way to Scillia's stables. He'd seen such before and hoped he was wrong about its origin, but he'd felt as though someone was lurking in the distance the last few times he'd come to visit Cicely and today's events had him on edge.

He'd chosen a different route to Reynold's. The path was overgrown and covered an array of various holes and snags Adam had set to capture small animals. He knew where they were and exactly where to step. If he was being followed, the individual behind him would have no clue and eventually would fall prey to one of the traps.

Adam picked up the pace and began moving faster. He was already late getting back to the plantation. He'd finished his tasks and raked the garden, but he still needed to get back before the *bwana* returned from their cattle runs. If he didn't, he'd miss the opportunity to feed and brush Jethro because the *bwana* would be in the stables and Adam made a point to be as far from where they gathered as possible.

Adam heard a loud snap and an accompanying scream. He did not stop. He pushed his leg as fast as it would move and began a quick trot towards the tree line. The individual behind him was stunned and at most may have twisted an ankle or a knee but they'd still be coming, and Adam needed to get out of sight and back to the plantation as quickly as possible.

As he cleared the forest, he saw the cooking fires from the slave quarters. Adam continued to move towards the barn. He did not see any of the *bwana* near the stables. He darted into the closest stall and picked a pitchfork from the wall. He moved across the floor towards Jethro's stall. Adam stopped before entering to catch his breath. He didn't want to spook the horse. He entered the stall and began cooing softly as he walked towards the animal. He took Jethro's reigns and led the horse to the edge of the stables where he could see the outside while brushing the horse down.

Adam positioned the horse in front of him and began slowly brushing the animal's hunches from top to bottom. He kept his eyes on the barnyard. As he moved around Jethro, he saw one of the slave master's younger son's hobble into view. The youngster was covered in leaves and was clearly favoring his right knee. Adam watched the boy limp his way to the big house before disappearing into the lavish doorway. Adam finished brushing Jethro. He pulled two carrots from his pocket and a couple of apples. He fed them to the horse, stroking the animal's nose while he ate. Adam led Jethro back to his stall. He pushed the pitchfork through the piles of hay and sifted the stacks along the floor to provide a fresh bed for the horse to rest on. In the distance, he could hear the *bwana* coming over the ridge. Adam completed his task, took one last look at Jethro, exited the barn and began walking slowly to his cabin.

Normally, Adam would have pulled off his shirt and breeches and changed into the night shirt Cicely had made for him. Tonight, he was too tired to change; his mind on what he'd seen in the barnyard. He moved over to the bed and bent down on his knees.

"Lawd. I have given you all I have. Evry day I wake up and call your name befoe I rise. Evry night, I call ya name befoe I close my eyes. I don't ask you for much of nothing. You supply what I need and I'm thankful. But now, Lawd, I'm askin' that ya please take care of Cicely and *Mwana*. Auntie, if ya listening, watch over them."

Adam got up from the floor and crawled into bed. He tossed and turned before rolling on his side and catching a memory of the first time he'd seen Cicely smile. Adam held onto that memory as he faded off to sleep.

*****

Adam woke up in a cold sweat; visions of shadowy figures reaching for him in the darkness. He lay on his back forcing the images away and trying to dispel the wad of cotton sitting around his brain. He sat up and pushed his legs over the side of the bed. He pressed his left leg onto the floor and stood up. The limb felt stiff and the bone ached.

Adam sensed the slightest hint of rain in the air. He moved around his tiny quarters and picked up the shirt Cicely had made for him. He ran a warm towel over his chest, arms, and face before pulling the garment over his head. It felt cool against his skin. He pushed the edge up to his nose and breathed deeply. The faintest hint of Cicely's aroma captured his senses and made him smile.

Adam pulled a skillet off the table and tossed in a few pieces of dried pork. He placed a pot of water on the flame and emptied the last of the hominy into the mixture. He listened to the sizzle of the ingredients and closed his eyes. He saw the shadowy figure standing behind the trees. As he moved around his cabin preparing for the day, he stopped to listen to the distant thunder. He absently rubbed the top of his thigh and flexed his leg. He sorted out his plans and how he'd proceed to make the most of the day before the rain started.

A streak of lighting lit up the landscape. Adam moved towards the door and looked out over the courtyard. He'd seen something in the corner of his vision; something that didn't belong. He stepped out the door but stayed close to the tiny structure. Reaching into his pocket, he fingered the metal spoon he'd sharpened and embedded in a block of wood he'd confiscated from Mr. Taftin's fire logs.

Nothing moved but the rustle of wind through the branches. Adam looked towards the barn; he saw the flicker of the lamp lights and the soft glow of the lanterns in each stall. There was no other movement. Instinctively, he kept moving. He needed to get to Jethro before the storm hit to attach the horse's eye guards to keep the animal calm. As he moved along the courtyard, he saw movement to his left. He did not react but moved into a slow trot towards the stables. He was certain he was being followed.

Adam entered the stables cautiously. He picked up a nearby pitchfork and pushed the tool out in front of him, making sure to keep his back to the stables. He made his way to Jethro. The horse neighed at his scent and pushed his nose out over the stall towards Adam's waiting hand.

"Easy, boy."

He untied the reins and slowly eased upon Jethro's back. The horse rocked back and forth awaiting Adam's next command. He pushed Jethro towards the entrance and stopped. The thunder was closer and the lightning more frequent. Adam grazed the landscape with his eyes, seeking that one shadow that would confirm his instincts. He pushed Jethro out into the courtyard and turned him towards the tree line. Lifting his head towards the sky, Adam felt the cool, moist air settle across his face. In an instant, he kicked the horse's side and sped off for the trees. Jethro pushed forward in the darkness with Adam low against his back. Adam stroked the animal's haunches, feeling the power flow through his fingers. In the distance, he heard the steady beat of additional horses behind him. He did not turn; he knew who was behind him. Adam felt Jethro straining against the reins; he let the horse loose and felt the wind rush across his face.

The men behind Adam had been taken by surprise. Adam was well ahead and moving fast. He was almost at the tree line. If he made it, the *bwana* would have a harder time keeping up. The rain had started and the occasional streaks of lightning lit up the landscape like a dark room. Adam stayed low; he did not want to give the *bwana* an easy target. He watched the trees approaching quickly and prayed that he'd make it to the interior before they got a good scope on him.

The leaves hit Adam's face as Jethro pushed into the forest. He pulled the reins hard to the left. Jethro swung around a huge oak tree headed for the river. Adam knew if he made it to the riverbank, he could move across the water's edge and hide out in one of the thousands of caves. The *bwana* had not brought the dogs. Without them, Adam would be harder to track in the darkness and rain.

His mind turned to Cicely. He'd not had time to prepare her. When he'd taken the horses and seen the headmaster's son, his worst fears had been confirmed. Several field hands had warned him the *bwana* had been tracking him. They'd taken an interest in the number of trips Adam had been making to town, especially when they'd discovered he was doing odd jobs for Mr. Taftin.

Taftin's family were known sympathizers and any Niggra caught in the crosshairs was under scrutiny, but Adam had taken the chance for Cicely's sake. When Scillia's attempt to negotiate his co-opt to her homestead had failed, Cicely had begged Adam to take her away so their son would be born free. For months, Adam had tried to plan how he'd get the two of them across the river to the series of roads that marked the Freedom Trails. He'd promised Cicely he'd find a way. Now, that was in jeopardy as he moved through the forest trying to escape the *bwana*.

Adam felt Jethro flinch underneath him. The horse pulled against the reins. Adam sensed the gunshot move over his back. The *bwanas* were using the lightening bursts to target him. He didn't have enough cover. He pulled Jethro up and to the right; the horse teetered and went down. Adam felt a rush of pain in his left leg, but he managed to jump free and hit the ground running. He pushed behind a tree and watched as Jethro moved away in the opposite direction.

Adam lay crouched beneath the bushes watching the horses fly by. If he was lucky, it would take them a moment to realize they were chasing an empty horse; that would give him time to conceal himself and hope he could cover his scent.

He lay still a moment, listening to the rain fall against the earth, the sound magnified by the adrenaline pulsing through his ears. He looked out over the landscape. Nothing moved. He pushed from underneath the brush and started running.

*****

The rain was coming down in a steady torrent. Adam shivered. The new shirt Cicely had given him was soaked through and through. He stepped around a puddle and continued to move through the darkness. He felt like he'd been running for hours, hoping he was moving in the right direction. Without adequate light, he couldn't be certain he wasn't traveling in circles. After several false starts, he'd looked up at the moon and determined that it was approximately three in the morning. He still had a few hours of darkness.

He stopped. Something in the distance had moved. Adam turned slowly and moved deeper into the bushes. He closed his eyes and listened. He heard breathing, something close. He sat still for a moment and then pushed out of the bushes headed towards the sound of the river. He heard leaves shuffling behind him and a muffled click. Adam felt his left leg throbbing; the blood coursing through the muscles as he willed it to move along the wet ground.

Phumph. Adam felt a sharp pain beneath his rib cage.

Phumph. There was another twinge between his shoulders.

Phumph. His legs flew from underneath him. He lay against the wet earth, face down, eyes closed. His mind pushed back to the moment in the meadow when he'd kissed Cicely and felt her weight on top of him. Adam reached out his hand and touched her cheek.

It was warm against his palm. Her eyes were closed, her lips pursed almost in a smile.

Adam felt the back of a boot slam down on his spine. A pair of hands rolled him over and pressed down on his chest. He felt himself lifted off the ground. He reached for Cicely's smile. She reached back and then all was dark.

*****

Joseph
Charleston, South Carolina

"Joseph! Joseph! Are you okay?"

Joseph opened his eyes. Keyth was standing over him; his parents on either side. Joseph tried to sit up but felt dizzy.

"Whoa. Take it easy."

Keyth helped him up and into one of the chairs.

"Here, baby. Drink."

Joseph took the glass of water and drained it. He looked at the small group around him and smiled.

"I'm okay. Just a little dizzy."

"You went down like a cow at the rodeo, son. One minute you were up, and then we looked around and you'd tipped over."

"Oh, God. I could have killed you." Mrs. Sorenson was beside herself.

"Doc told you we needed to cut back on the sugar," Mr. Sorenson bellowed with a slight smile.

"No. No. I'm fine. It wasn't the food. All of a sudden, I felt lightheaded. I'm okay. Really. Please, can I have another glass of water? I feel fine. Honestly."

Mrs. Sorenson rose slowly, accompanied by her husband; the two disappeared into the house.

"Yo, man. You sure you're okay? You came down pretty hard." Keyth sat next to Joseph with a look of concern.

"I'm fine. Could be the heat. Could be all this good home cooking or a combination of both. I am not certain, but I'm okay, seriously."

"Aight. But I'mma keep my eye on you in case you've decided to stay and try to take over my room or something." Keyth slapped Joseph on the shoulder and left to join his parents.

Joseph watched Keyth disappear into the kitchen. He eased to the edge of the chair and attempted to stand but felt the floor move. He placed his hands in his lap and quietly sat back in the safety of the armchair. Despite the heat, he felt a chill run across his back. He knew what the vision meant. He understood what had happened yet he still felt connected. He still felt Adam's presence. He needed to get to his journal, but more importantly, he needed to find the truth.

*****

Dakar, Senegal

Joseph lay in bed listening to Taylor breathe. It had been a long week. They'd spent time exploring Goree Island, recovering items in hopes of matching them with kinsfolk. He'd transported her there to ensure that her empathic link to Cicely was capped but in doing so, he'd found himself revisiting his peculiar links to the past; rehashing memories he'd allowed to lay dormant or pushed aside for other pursuits. Joseph had also informed Taylor of his plans to relocate. He'd sensed her trepidation. After years of confusion and uncertainty, it was difficult to commit to the idea of normalcy, but he'd absolved her fears, at least momentarily.

Joseph ran his hand along the contours of her naked frame. She moaned softly but did not wake. He loved watching her sleep and felt an abundance of joy seeing her at peace. He kissed the back of her neck, snuggled into her warmth and closed his eyes.

On the edge of sleep, Joseph saw another face smiling at him. He reached out his hand, touched her cheek and whispered her name.

Taylor moved beneath Joseph's arm. She rolled over to face him and kissed him on the tip of his nose.

"You okay?"

"Did I wake you?"

"It's not as if you have a motion sensitive mattress." Taylor smiled.

"I'm sorry."

"What's on your mind?"

"I need to find Adam's family."

"I thought you gave up when you finished your studies."

"Not wholly. Each trip to the States, I gather more information. My last venture, I hired a genealogist. She found a road map to the participants on the railroad in Charleston."

Taylor reached out and touched Joseph's face. He kissed her fingertips and squeezed her hand in his own before pulling her into his arms.

"How far have you gotten?"

"I found Lee and Elizabeth; the husband and wife that moved Matthew and Elijah on the railroad."

"And from there, where do you hope to go?"

"If I can piece together the network, I might be able to trace the boys to their final destinations and from there, who knows."

"You are setting yourself up for an extensive journey into a bottomless rabbit hole."

"I need to do this."

Taylor looked up from Joseph's arms. "Why? What do you hope to gain?"

"I'm not certain, but it feels necessary. Do I sound completely crazy?"

"No. You don't sound crazy, but you have to accept that you may not find a happy ending."

Joseph rubbed his hand along Taylor's back. He closed his eyes and allowed her heat to seep into his doubts.

"Helping you through your ordeal with Cicely made me realize that their lives matter. I've been a part of Adam's journey for most of my life, and I have a responsibility to finish his story; to give it meaning and to make it relevant. Please tell me you understand."

"I understand, but I worry you'll lose faith if you can't find what you're seeking, or that the story itself will hurt you. You're three generations removed. You're speculating that his brothers survived, that they weren't captured or worse. There are a lot of unknowns, Joseph."

"I have faith, Tay. I have to. Being with you has shown me that much. I promise that if my efforts do not reveal any viable leads, I will cease, but I must try."

Taylor kissed Joseph and snuggled in his arms. She yawned unceremoniously.

"I believe you, baby. But for now, can we sleep?"

Joseph laughed. "Yes, love. Rest."

Joseph felt Tay's warmth surround him. He closed his eyes and prayed. Soon, he too was sound asleep.

*****

Philadelphia, Pennsylvania

Joseph maneuvered through traffic watching for the alley that led to Pagent Donaldson's office. He spotted the crossroad and clicked the turn signal. He ignored the honking horns and belligerent rants as he made his way across the lanes towards the quaint little nook off the main road, tucked on the side of a boulevard in what used to be a duplex.

He and Taylor separated at the airport after their journey from Ghana. Tay's flight to Charleston left first, and Joseph utilized his layover to peruse the documents Pagent had compiled from her research. He anticipated the exchange yet felt apprehensive about the outcome; the unspoken "what next?"

Joseph parked, pulled the keys from the ignition, and sat quietly. He watched two squirrels, listened to the melody from the birds singing nearby and watched a couple push their toddler down the sidewalk.

In this instant, life was uncomplicated. He was preparing to relocate. He'd transitioned the bulk of his research to various scholars and interns on his resident team while assuming responsibility for the majority of Jackson's studies in Oklahoma. He and Taylor had spent their time together discussing the future, and Joseph felt sure of his plans to propose when the two reunited in Charleston. For all intents and purposes, Joseph's life was where he'd dreamed it could be that day in the jeep when he and his family left their homestead and attempted to start over.

Yet his mind kept rewinding Taylor's "Why?" After everything she'd been through, she should have understood his motivation, yet he could not fault her for distressing. He'd dismissed the significance of Adam's life until he'd met her, and in that moment, realized fate had placed her in his path to reconnect him. Thus, there had to be a reason for his search. There was no guarantee his efforts would reveal anything more than he'd fathomed from his shadowy memories, but he owed it to the universe to try.

*****

"Good afternoon, Mr. Iglaysia. Very nice to meet you. Please, have a seat."

"Thank you, Ms. Donaldson. I am encouraged by what you've sent me thus far. The documents appear to be in excellent condition."

"Yes. The record keeping for the period is normally not as pristine. We were definitely lucky."

Ms. Donaldson retrieved a large folder from her desk and began spreading documents out on top. Some, Joseph had already seen; others were familiar but had not been disclosed. Ms. Donaldson meticulously distributed them in neat stacks before pushing a set in front of Joseph to read.

"What you have there are the first cataloged slave census records for the state. You can see from the manifest there are several slaves named Adam. However, only three fit the description you gave me. Male. Aged seventeen to twenty. I was able to locate four properties under the name Reynolds. Unfortunately, none of the males registered are specifically listed on the asset rosters for these particular properties. That is not unusual, however, without a direct connection, I can't link any of the males to a distinct homestead or plantation."

Ms. Donaldson picked up a second folder and placed it in front of Joseph.

"Here are the medical records listing a physician named Lee Britton. Initially, he was recorded as the town medical consultant in Cayce, South Carolina. There is no record of an Elizabeth until five years later. It appears Mr. Britton married Ms. Elizabeth Montigue in Aiken, South Carolina. The couple set up residence on a homestead in Cayce two years later. The couple have no children on record although registers mention a burial three years after the pair moved to Cayce."

Joseph waited while the woman retrieved a third folder. She opened it and spread the contents out in front of him.

"The Britons are listed among the defendants in a case brought to the Charleston officials regarding the acquisition of properties solely possessed by several plantation owners in various parts of the Carolinas. The court documents list several names in conjunction with this suit."

Ms. Donaldson retrieved a map from the back of the folder. The drawing contained several highlighted routes.

"A comparison of this map to those names reveals that each is located at some juncture along one of these routes. From this and a second map located in the archives, I deduced that these individuals were participating in a branch of the Underground Railroad initially established in the South during the early stages of the Spanish occupation.

"The deliberations of the trial lasted two weeks. Several plantation owners came forward with complaints but with no viable evidence against any of the defendants. As a result, each were found not guilty and released. Mr. and Mrs. Britton were among those defendants."

Joseph listened intently. "Do we have any idea who might have been the main conductor?"

Ms. Donaldson pulled out her notebook and flipped through several pages. Joseph sat quietly looking through the documents as the woman perused her notes.

"Several court documents reference one defendant on four separate occasions regarding the same complaint. Josiah Yueling. A homesteader that moved from New York to Charleston in his early thirties."

Ms. Donaldson picked up the map and circled three plots along the highlighted routes.

"Mr. Yueling is listed as the owner for each of these properties. As you can see, they are located at various intervals near the border and what some suspect may have been the exchange for travelers."

"Are there any eyewitness accounts?"

"There are several publications that identify Mr. Yueling by name in various capacities regarding public meetings related to the Freedman's Marches. Tracing the lineage, there is a Jeremiah Yueling listed as a Union Soldier of some rank in several battles along the East Coast. A Melissa Yueling mentioned as an advocate during the Jim Crow era. There are various sporadic mentions of the name in relation to other civil or domestic causes, but the final bit of evidence is a post humus autobiography written by Mr. Yueling's great-great-great-grandson, Donovan, that may be of interest to you."

Ms. Donaldson pulled out a hardback book and placed it on the table between them. She opened the book to a page that had several highlighted passages. Joseph read the first paragraph and looked up at Ms. Donaldson with a smile.

"This was written by Mr. Yueling's grandson."

"Yes, sir. From what I can decipher, the book is based on stories told by various family members from personal accounts with Mr. Yueling or from other sources closely involved with his business."

"May I keep this copy?"

"Yes, sir. I purchased the biography on your behalf."

"Is there anything else?"

"Not at the moment. I have a few additional leads for which I am awaiting feedback. Contingent on the information, I will be in touch."

Joseph stood and shook the older lady's hand before bending to give her a kiss on the cheek. The gesture caught her off guard. For a moment she looked confused, but it soon gave way to a huge smile and a slight tinge of rose to her cheeks.

"I greatly appreciate your due diligence in this endeavor, Ms. Donaldson. Rest assured, you will be hearing from me on any additional projects for which your services will be an asset. Thank you again."

Joseph sat in the front seat of the rental car with a huge smile on his face. Pagent had collected more information than he could have hoped, and to have a written account of what could potentially be movements along the railroads through Charleston was invaluable. He picked up his cellphone and tapped the Travelocity app. He needed to book a flight and schedule a meeting with Mr. Yueling.

*****

Manchester, New Hampshire

"Hello. Mr. Yueling? My name's Joseph Iglaysia. We spoke on the phone this morning."

Joseph reached out to shake the gentleman's hand extended towards him. Donovan Yueling was in his late sixties, but either through an excellent set of genomes or an expensive plastic surgeon, the man could have easily passed for half his age. He stood approximately 6'5" with a full head of salt-and-pepper hair clipped in an efficient military buzz cut. Joseph returned the steel grip that passed between them and smiled.

"Nice to meet you, Mr. Iglaysia. I am pleased that you've taken an interest in my book, albeit I am uncertain how I might be able to shed light on your search. Please, have a seat. Would you like some coffee or something stronger, perhaps?"

"I would love a cup of coffee. Thank you."

Joseph watched the man move around a small table and turned over two large mugs.

"My grandchildren bought me this Mr. Coffee for Christmas. I'm a staunch coffee snob. Before my wife and I moved here, I'd get up every morning and grind the beans by hand for our first cup of coffee. It was a rite of passage my father passed down to each of his children. I opened this box and swore it would never get used."

Joseph smiled as Mr. Yueling poured a cup of grinds in the device's tray and pushed it closed. There was a soft hissing sound followed by the pungent aroma of fresh coffee.

"What's your poison?"

"Unsweetened with a touch of cream."

Donovan handed Joseph a mug and a small pitcher filled with cream. He waited for Joseph to season the brew to taste and returned the pitcher to the table before completing his own cup and taking a seat next to him. The two men savored the moment before easing into the subject of discussion.

"You're interested in my grandfather's stories?"

"Yes, sir. I am attempting to trace a group of boys that I believe passed through your grandfather's properties."

"Grandfather Yueling hosted a lot of parties in his day." Donovan smiled. "He was active in the trade until he passed away in 1851. I could not imagine that type of stress at ninety-eight years old. But when you believe in something, I suppose that's the only reason you need to rise in the morning."

"What was it like hearing your grandparents recount their stories?"

"I am ashamed to admit that my siblings and I took their time for granted for the majority of our youth. It is the curse of each generation to discount the importance of oral traditions especially in this age of electronic communication and push button conveniences."

Joseph smiled attempting to imagine life without his Blackberry and iPhone.

"My wife and I host Thanksgiving. A few years back, we initiated a 'Family Only Holiday.' The premise is that anyone that enters our house is required to engage in a face-to-face conversation with another family member for the duration of the visit.

"It was a tough sell in the beginning. It took a while, but eventually everyone got onboard. Now, it's a time we look forward to and one that my wife and I cherish as we watch the children grow. It is a moment to reflect on family and share our history."

Joseph sipped his coffee and pondered his nostalgic feelings for his own family.

"What made you write the book?"

"Grandfather's stories have a ring of truth; they're alive and vibrant with the characters and emotions of the time. My humanities' professor was impressed by the anthology I submitted for a final. He encouraged me to enter an essay contest. I won second place and netted the attention of a publisher serving as a visiting judge. He suggested I write a book. At the time, I was young, in college, and living with my parents. I kept his card and moved on.

"Years later, well beyond middle age, I started a reading club at my church. I'd never considered publishing Grandfather's legacy, but I was amazed at the subject matter that found its way to the top ten. It so happened that in the same year, I broke my back in two places. I was immobile and irritable. My wife, for the sake of our marriage and her sanity, bought me a dictaphone. The rest is history, literally."

"Were the narratives difficult to corroborate?"

"The Gullah revere oral tradition; there are individuals that function as orators even in this modern age. I have several contacts that provide insight towards projects they are initiating and who are linked with the Charleston City Council to cultivate a way to preserve these voices.

"Grandfather was a huge figure in the area. I spent several years verifying the historical landmarks, coupled with census records. But the preponderance of my research began with the oral accounts from my family and those validated by sources in the region."

Mr. Yueling stood. He reached for Joseph's cup and refilled both before reclaiming his seat.

"Those were interesting times. People were of one mind or the other. Grandfather was never one to follow the crowd. He was a self-made man that didn't owe his fortunes to anything but hard work, so it was not a surprise that he chose to buck societal caprices." Donovan paused, lost in thought before smiling and turning his attention back to Joseph. "My apologies. You're not here to reminisce. How can I help you?"

"I'm interested in one particular story."

Joseph opened Mr. Yueling's book to the section about his Grandfather's first encounter with the Charleston Bounty Hunters.

"It says here that your Grandfather hid the slaves in his gun shed when the Bounty Hunters arrived. They searched the entire property and never found anything. Mr. Yueling knew they'd set a scout to watch his movements, so he devised a plan to move the slaves before his window of opportunity closed."

"My brothers and I spent every summer with my grandparents on Grandfather Yueling's homestead. We'd spend the entire time searching the tunnels scattered around the property. When the inheritance passed to me, I commissioned a team of surveyors to create a comprehensive map including the tunnels."

Donovan rose from his chair and walked to a small cabinet. He opened a drawer and hauled out a large plastic shell. He returned and spread the map out on the table in front of Joseph.

"As the auctions gained traction, the slave catchers began patrolling the rivers for runaways. They knew the quickest and least detectable routes were by boat. Grandfather's crew devised the means to get slaves to destinations downstream; areas where the Chattooga River branched off into small tributaries that could be navigated inland." Donovan pointed out several markers on the map. "Here, here, and here are points where Grandfather stored kayaks for transport. Here, here, and here are points where he used local trappers with larger boats."

"Wasn't that dangerous?"

"The men that worked with my grandfather were loyal. Each had either grown up with him or worked for his father at some point in their lives. These men made their living on the river. Their allegiance was to the almighty dollar and Grandfather's pockets ran deeper than most."

"Who dug the tunnels?"

"The slaves. For every batch of men and women that were brought to the trails, most had a hand in creating the system you see here. Some would stay hidden for months digging and fortifying the tunnels until they reached the rivers and streams. In return, Grandfather took care of them."

Donovan pulled out another set of documents and passed them to Joseph.

"My parents gave this to my wife and me when we married. It's a manifesto Grandfather wrote a few years before he died. It lists several key servants and farmhands as beneficiaries to parcels of land he owned throughout South Carolina. I discovered that many of these individuals were sold at auction to slave owners in other states. There are no formal records of Grandfather ever purchasing or owning slaves under his homestead, so I assume they arrived looking for freedom and never left."

Joseph sat quietly taking in all the information.

"Did your grandfather keep records, notes, anything that would provide an account of the individuals that passed through the property?"

"I've yet to discover documentation of that nature. We petitioned to have certain buildings on the property remodeled. Working with the historical society, we discovered there'd been a house fire. My assumption is that many of the documents Grandfather might have kept were probably lost in that incident. The closest I've found are court certificates citing slaves Grandfather was accused of pilfering, but these are few and far between. However…"

Donovan rummaged through his pile of notes. He thumbed through several notebooks before handing Joseph a yellowed sheet of paper with a list of names.

"My brothers and I found this one evening in the tunnel leading from the main house. The atmosphere is surprisingly arid. Those conditions are most likely the only reason that document still exists. I am not certain, but I believe it's a collation of the individuals in the network. I'm working to confirm that premise, but to date, my efforts have been less than stellar."

Joseph scanned the page. As he critiqued the names, his mind settled on L. E. Britton and several others that appeared to match those he'd seen in Philadelphia. Joseph pulled out his bundle of documents and handed Donovan, Pagent's list. He watched as the man's face morphed into a broad smile.

"I assumed the letters were initials. I never considered they represented a husband and wife. I've spent the last year trying to put those names with individuals in the region. How did you come by this?"

"My resource pulled court documents and compared similar cases with your grandfather's. From those, she compiled this list of potential cohorts, or at the very least, individuals that were equally complicit."

"Amazing. Might I have a copy?"

"Of course. If I can make a similar request for the manifesto?"

"You may keep that particular copy. The original is in an exhibition along with other family documents and heirlooms. My wife and I discovered while dating that we share an affinity for history. Being of like mind, we've dedicated our meager resources to preserving our respective family's antiquities. Our goal is to be remembered, but most importantly to engender in our grandchildren and their children the importance of heritage and history. What is man without his past?"

Joseph stood and extended his hand to Mr. Yueling. "I truly appreciate your time. I have enjoyed speaking with you."

Donovan shook Joseph's hand with a broad smile.

"I have enjoyed the occasion also. I seldom have opportunities to discuss my family's history with individuals outside kinsmen. It is a joy to share with someone who hasn't heard every rendition my siblings and I can put together."

"On that note, would you be interested in coming to New York for a seminar? A colleague and I are working on a symposium to highlight the Middle Passage; not in the traditional sense but through the eyes of the descendants. I'd very much appreciate your input regarding stories from third party constituents as well."

"I would be honored. Please let me know when, and I will adjust my schedule accordingly."

Joseph extended his hand again. "Thank you, Mr. Yueling. It has been a pleasure."

*****

Cayce, South Carolina

Joseph joined Taylor in Charleston after his trip to New Hampshire. The two spent the next few days with Taylor's grandmother and parents talking over plans and celebrating their recent engagement.

Taylor's grandmother was ecstatic about the news. Joseph wasn't as certain about Taylor's parents. Each seemed happy enough, but Joseph got the impression Taylor's father was less than amenable to the idea. To his delight, Taylor either hadn't noticed or didn't care, but he suspected there was a conversation to be had.

Joseph and Taylor rode together in silence as he maneuvered through the heavy traffic towards the destination the guide highlighted on the map. Joseph was lost in his thoughts. He looked over at Taylor and smiled; her head rolling gently around the headrest while she slept. He returned his eyes to the road and let his mind revisit the conversation with Donovan Yueling.

For the first time in months, Joseph had a solid lead. If he was fortunate, there might be additional information or at least another clue. He was hopeful. He pushed past a pick-up truck and swerved to avoid missing his turn. Doing so, he woke Taylor.

"Hey. I didn't sign up for a roller coaster ride."

"Sorry, baby."

"Are we there yet?" Taylor smiled.

"Another eight miles or so down this road, and I believe we will be."

"I'm glad we came early. This is not downtown Charleston for sho."

"You're not afraid of a little country are you?" Joseph smiled.

Taylor stuck out her tongue and unfolded the map in her lap.

"It shows that we're about here. Not too far from the state line but a good ways inland."

"By car, it seems short. Imagine the trip on foot, in dense forest with nothing but moonlight, if that."

"Point taken."

The road was narrow and covered in loose gravel. The wheels rolled over it gingerly as Joseph continued towards the imaginary "X" in his head. As they moved along, Taylor saw moss-covered buildings behind newly renovated structures. She noted a liquor store in front of what appeared to be a moonshine still. She smiled at the irony. As the trees parted, they noticed a small church next to a group of old wagons. There appeared to be a wedding taking place as the bridesmaids and grooms stood in line awaiting their cue to enter.

"We could probably rent the church for little or nothing," Taylor quipped from the passenger seat.

"You joke, but that may not be such a bad idea after flying my family here from Kenya."

"We could always have the ceremony in Africa. My parents and grandmother have always thought of visiting. We could make it a family affair."

"I had not thought of that. What about the rest of your family? Your friends?"

"Outside of the individuals you've met and Professor V, there's not anyone that would be overtly snubbed. It's not like I'm a social butterfly or nothing."

Joseph laughed. He rounded a corner and pushed the car up a small hill. When they topped the ridge, he could see the outlines of a house and several adjoining buildings. He inched closer and saw the house coming into view. He pushed the car forward and listened to the engine hum up the hilly terrain. He stopped a few feet away and turned off the car.

"There it is. The house where Lee and Elizabeth Britton lived."

They exited the car and stood side-by-side as if in anticipation of some unspoken summons. Sensing Joseph's trepidation, Taylor took his hand in hers and gave it a gentle squeeze.

"We're here. Now what?"

"The curator said the parcels are occupied by custodians familiar with the chronological facts of the property. The majority are either descendants of the owners or stewards responsible for the thoroughfare's conservancy."

"Hello!"

They watched a tall gentleman approaching from one of the smaller buildings.

"Can I help you?" He walked up to them quickly and extended his hand to Joseph then Taylor.

"Name's Briton, Virgil. And you are?"

"Joseph Iglaysia."

"Greetings, Mr. Iglaysia. Donovan mentioned you might arrive for a visit."

"Word travels fast."

"It does indeed. You're interested in touring the property?"

"Yes. If I may. I am not certain what I'm looking for, but I'd like to hear the history."

Joseph ran through his notes and broached the question at the forefront of his thoughts; recalling that Pagent had mentioned the Briton's had no children.

"You mentioned your last name is Briton. Are you related to the family?"

"My mother was the great-great-grandniece of the original homesteader. She died of cancer a few years back. She was devoted to the preservation of her family's homestead. After her death, the rights passed to my family."

"My condolences for your loss."

"Thank you." The man seemed solemn for a moment before reengaging and leading them to a small shed at the back of the property.

"I suppose this will be as good a spot as any to start. Donovan told me to give you the ins and outs, not the tourist version, so if you have questions, please do not hesitate to inquire."

The three moved around the property stopping at small buildings or enclosures. At each point, Virgil relayed some tidbit about the family's history. As they neared the lower end of the property, Joseph spotted a small graveyard sequestered in the trees.

"Is that the family plot?"

"Yes."

"Can we take a closer look?"

"Of course."

The three walked along the trail leading to the gravestones. The plot was poorly maintained. Joseph suspected as a means of deterring patrons from frequenting the area. As they moved closer, Joseph noticed three headstones. The presence of a third seemed odd considering he had not noted any additional members of the Briton family in South Carolina. As they moved closer, he could clearly see the chiseled names of Lee Briton and Elizabeth Briton on their respective markers. As he knelt down to take a closer look at the third, his heart stopped. Across the top in crude lettering was the name Matthew. He placed his hand on the cool stone and said a silent prayer.

"Did the Briton's have a child?"

"Unfortunately no. Elizabeth experienced a severe case of scarlet fever in her teens. As a result, she was unable to bear children. She and Lee took several orphans into their home, many of which continue to serve as benefactors for the homestead, but they had no natural children of their own."

"Who is buried here?"

"As the story goes. A group of Negro boys found their way to the homestead one night in a storm." Virgil smiled. "Contingent on who's telling the tale, there were four, some say twelve. Estimated guess, there were at least eight. The youngest was probably four. The oldest appeared to be twelve. They took the children in, fed them, and placed them in the basement of their home. Lee was almost certain that a hunting party would not be far behind. As it so happened, several men arrived the next day inquiring."

Taylor watched Joseph stand. He looked in her direction, but she could tell by the tilt of his head that he did not see her. She watched him closely as Virgil continued to speak, noting the tension in his shoulders and the steady rise and fall of his chest. She heard alarms in her head but she did not move to intervene. She trusted Joseph to know his limits.

"Elizabeth was an avid reader and she enjoyed writing. There are several of her short stories and journals on display in the main house. There is one entry that appears to coincide with the story of the Negro boys.

"She speaks of an incident where one of the boys left the house to go to the barn. Understandably, she was paralyzed with fear that he'd be discovered and that she and Lee would be hanged.

"The men had an adolescent male slave with them. He'd been badly injured. Lee was the town doctor and with some persuasion, he and Elizabeth convinced the men to allow them to attend to the slave's wounds. Apparently, the young man who'd left the house was the brother of the slave who'd been hurt. Lee did what he could for the slave and soon the hunters went on their way. Sensing that an element of danger remained, the Briton's kept the boys hidden until they could move them safely to the next check point.

"Over the course of the stay, the young one who'd left the house became ill. Elizabeth notes he had a high fever and was unable to keep anything on his stomach. One of the younger boys would not leave his side. With some coaxing, they learned each of the boy's names. Matthew was the child who'd become sick. The young one that would not leave him was his brother, Elijah.

"Despite their best efforts, Lee and Elizabeth were unable to save Matthew. By best guess, Lee determined he'd died from dysentery. Being good Christian folk, they buried him here."

Joseph had stopped breathing. The ringing in his ears was deafening as he watched Virgil's lips continue to move. The ground beneath his feet was shifting. The trees around him seemed to be shrinking. He turned to look at Matthew's headstone a few inches from his hand. He reached out to touch it and felt the heat of Taylor's grip surround him. He looked up into her worried eyes. She reached out and touched his chest. He exhaled, the air struggling to reach his lungs as his mind forced its way back into the moment.

"You okay, Mr. Iglaysia?"

Joseph took a deep breath and squeezed Taylor's hand to assure her that he was okay.

"I'm fine. You mention Matthew's brother, Elijah. Do you know what happened to him?"

"Dysentery is infectious. Elijah contracted a milder case. Lee separated the others, and when it was safe, took them to the next point; Elizabeth stayed behind to nurse the two. With Matthew gone and the remaining boys scattered, Elijah had no one. So Lee and Elizabeth raised him here on the homestead."

"Here? In South Carolina?"

"Yes, sir. He's referenced in several of Elizabeth's journals."

Joseph needed to sit down. His throat was dry and his head felt as though it were going to jump from his shoulders. He bent his knees and took a hand full of the gravel surrounding Matthew's grave. He sifted through the debris and selected two nice stones. Tossing the rest aside, he pushed the stones into his pocket and returned his attention to Virgil Briton.

"I'd like to see those journals, if possible, and any other information you have related to the children."

"Certainly. If you'll follow me. I can take you to the display we have set aside in the main house."

"We will follow momentarily. I'd like a minute alone with my fiancée."

"Of course. Take your time."

Joseph watched Virgil leave. He waited until he was down the hill and moving towards the house before pulling Taylor into an embrace. He held her close, burying his confusion in her scent, attempting to grapple with the thoughts racing through his mind. She rested against his frame, trying to anticipate what he needed. She kissed the inside of his neck and spoke softly against his ear.

"Are you okay?"

Joseph released her, placing his hand on her cheek. He smiled. He had no words, no plan. He was reconciling the fact that he'd found Adam's brothers. He'd laid hands on the place where Matthew rested and potentially stood to discover what had become of Elijah as well. It was humbling. He'd spent the majority of his life with someone else's thoughts, and here he stood with the evidence of their existence in front of him.

"Yes. A bit overwhelmed, but I'm fine."

Joseph turned and looked down at Matthew's headstone.

"They buried him. They tried to save him, and then they buried him here on their land. They took in Elijah and raised him. They were good people in a vat of evil. Why do people like that disappear? Where do they go?"

"The world's not ending, Joseph."

"Not for you and I, but for Adam and the rest of those children, they never had peace. They grew up in chaos. No one deserves that. No one should have to live without hope."

Taylor understood. Joseph was voicing his doubts and memories from a time when he'd been terrified and uncertain. She took his hand and led him to a small bench beneath a large tree. Sitting next to him, she listened. Offering solace but mostly allowing him to vent, to release everything he'd suppressed since that night in the tunnel—the fear and worry, the angst, and frustration. He'd never screamed or forgiven the nine-year-old boy that had been afraid and blamed himself.

Joseph talked until the light began to fade against the horizon. Virgil had come up the hill with two Styrofoam containers of food and cups of iced tea. He'd informed them that the grounds were closing for the evening, but that they were welcome to return to tour the house and Elizabeth's journals. He also gave Joseph a business card with the name and number of the lawyer that handled the Briton Foundation's trust. He informed that Mr. Dilligence would be a viable resource for locating any of Elijah Briton's descendants. Joseph twirled the card between his fingers while Taylor maneuvered through traffic.

"I appreciate your coming with me today."

"Where else would I have been?"

"You could have gone back to Texas with your parents or stayed behind with your grandmother."

"G-Mama would have talked my ears off and my parents need some time."

Joseph smiled. "So I wasn't imagining things."

"My parents are very protective. I think they'd given up on my having a 'normal' life. Granted, I haven't done much to foster any confidence in such. After many failed attempts at relationships or simply human contact, they stopped asking. Now to consider marriage and the prospect of grandchildren after years of wondering if I'd merely survive—it's a lot."

"Should I be worried?"

"No. Mom will warm up to the prospect of spending money, pretty dresses and most definitely the idea of my having to conform to makeup and a dress…OMG, she will never stop taking pictures. Daddy. He and I are going to have to talk."

"Sounds serious."

"He's been my gladiator forever. That's not a title he's going to relinquish without some coercion."

"I come in peace, and I'm equally vested."

Taylor laughed. The two rode together in silence while Joseph attempted to make sense of everything he'd just found. His mind was racing. His thoughts cloudy as he attempted to put the pieces together and determine what next. As they entered the lobby, the concierge called to them.

"Good afternoon. We received a message for Mr. Iglaysia."

The gentleman handed Joseph a blue notecard with a name and phone number. Joseph did not recognize the number. He and Taylor returned to their room. Taylor resumed packing their things while Joseph dialed the number on the card.

"Hello."

"Mr. Iglaysia?"

"Yes. With whom am I speaking?"

"My name is Ayreal Montgomery. I am Elijah Briton's granddaughter."

Joseph motioned for Taylor to come over. He put the phone on speaker as the two sat listening to the woman on the other end.

"Virgil called this afternoon and informed that you were at the Briton homestead inquiring about my uncle and grandfather's history."

"Yes, ma'am. I appreciate your call."

"It is my pleasure. We entertain so few inquiries into the nuances of the individual lives. Many visit for the novelty, few seldom want to know more. I am intrigued by your query. How can I assist?"

Joseph sat mesmerized, uncertain how to respond.

"I'm open to anything you have to offer."

"How long are you going to be in Charleston?"

"We are visiting family under no particular time constraints."

"Excellent. I'm going to send reservations for a flight to my home in Toronto. I have something I want to show you."

"Yes, ma'am. I look forward to speaking with you."

*****

Toronto, Canada

Joseph sat in the back of a GMC Yukon en route to Ayreal Montgomery's estate. Following the instructions she'd forwarded, he'd arrived at the airport to find a first-class ticket, the number to a limo service and a room reservation.

The night before, he and Taylor had continued to work through the emotional aftermath from their visit to the Briton homestead. Joseph had not realized the extent of his anger. Had he been diagnosing a patient, he would have likened his response to survivor's guilt. He blamed himself for the events in his past and was somehow using his quest to find Adam's brothers as recompense. Despite Joseph's insistence, Taylor convinced him that the remaining journey was something he needed to undertake alone to confront and reconcile his feelings.

The SUV stopped in front of a gated entrance. Joseph rolled down the window as the apparatus swung open. The vehicle pulled forward revealing an expanse of land peppered with northern red oaks, sugar maples, and perfectly manicured grass. The driver pushed the SUV slowly up the driveway, but to Joseph's surprise, did not stop at the main house but continued around back to a smaller building.

The man exited the vehicle and opened Joseph's door. He led Joseph to the entrance of the building, knocked and awaited a response. A tall dark-skinned male appeared and offered his hand to Joseph. The two exchanged a firm handshake. The gentleman briefly addressed the driver before leading Joseph into the interior of the space.

"Nice to meet you, Mr. Iglaysia. I'm Jersey Montgomery, Ayreal Montgomery's son. I'm the curator here."

"Pardon my asking, but where is here?"

"You're standing in the middle of the Elijah Britton Artistic Study Museum."

"Museum?" Joseph was flabbergasted. "How?"

Jersey smiled. "Follow me. Mother's waiting in the garden. I'll let her explain."

Joseph followed the man through the building to a set of double doors. They stepped through into a large back yard. Seated under a gazebo in the middle of the property was an older woman. She sat comfortably with her hands crossed in her lap and a phone propped against one ear. As they moved closer, Joseph could hear her speaking.

Jersey leaned in and kissed her on the cheek; she smiled and squeezed his hand. Jersey motioned for Joseph to approach. Ms. Montgomery returned his handshake and gestured for him to take a seat. Jersey turned and walked away, leaving the two alone.

A servant appeared from the house carrying a tray of tea and pastries. Another appeared with water and lemons. Both bowed and retraced their steps to the house. Ms. Montgomery motioned for Joseph to help himself while she completed her call.

"No sir. The drawing in question is not for auction. It has been donated to a local high school for study and there is no negotiable price. Should you choose to display the piece, my son will be happy to work out a contract; otherwise, we have no additional business to discuss. I appreciate your time." Ms. Montgomery returned the receiver to its cradle before placing the phone on the table between them.

"Mr. Iglaysia. A pleasure to meet you. My apologies for the delay. We are negotiating with the various art houses. It is a cumbersome process I have yet to fully relinquish to Jersey."

"No worries. What is this place?"

Ms. Montgomery reached for a cup of tea. She doctored the elixir and sat thoughtfully before speaking.

"This is my family's estate. My father, Ezekiel Britton, inherited the property from his father, Abram. It was passed to Abram from his father, Peter, who received the land from grandfather, Elijah. As Ezekiel's oldest heir, the property and museum are now under my care. When I retire, the onus shall pass to my youngest, Jersey."

"It is a beautiful estate."

Ms. Montgomery smiled. "It is a labor of love. Here in Toronto, we have this estate, a financial firm, and various auxiliary endeavors. My uncles and aunts have established investment firms, educational trusts, political activist campaigns and various humanitarian platforms throughout the United States and abroad. My siblings and cousins are all engaged in some aspect of the family's holdings."

"Venerable endeavors. I'm certain Elijah would be pleased."

"One would hope."

Joseph sat quietly. He sensed there was more to the Briton legacy but he chose not to pry; familial finances were often analogous to politics—corrupt and merciless.

Ayreal took a sip of tea and smiled. "Donovan explains that you're attempting to trace grandfather's history."

"I was surprised to hear that the Britons raised Elijah in their home. Considering the environment and the politics, I can imagine it would have been a challenge."

"I've read Elizabeth's journals. She and Lee were a unique couple. He was the abolitionist; she became such through attrition: love the man, tolerate the vision. The ideology became less of an intrusion when she recognized that many of these children were entering their new lives as orphans. At that juncture, having no children but needing to nurture, she became a surrogate. My grandfather was the first of many that would grow up in her home.

"As children, we were told the story of how Grandfather and Uncle crossed the river to find the Briton house. The story never grows old and with each generation it takes on a different connotation.

"Jersey has taken it upon himself to record a version for our archives; he's also transcribed an account for print. We hope to have it published along with several of Grandfather's paintings, perhaps as a children's book or short story."

"Elijah became an artist?"

Ayreal laughed, a hearty sound that echoed through the nearby trees.

"My apologies. I must remember the reason for your query." She stood. "Follow me."

Joseph pushed up from his seat and fell in step behind Aryeal. The two walked towards a small set of doors. Aryeal opened them and stepped aside for Joseph to enter. They were in a large, dark room. She reached for a remote attached to an adjacent wall, aimed the apparatus at a small box and pushed. Joseph heard a low hum and then watched as the curtains covering the windows retracted revealing the full scope of the space. As natural light filled the room, Joseph could see pictures lining the walls.

"Welcome to the Elijah Briton collection."

Joseph saw various sized pictures lining the walls. There were landscapes, portraits, abstracts, seascapes. From end to end, all he could see were paintings.

"Elijah painted all these?"

"In this room. We have others comprised of renditions he did of artists he studied with or tutored."

Joseph walked up and down the corridors. He stopped in front of each painting, taking in the colors and subject matter. He assumed most were of Elijah's life—places he'd been, individuals he'd encountered.

"These are amazing. How is this possible?"

"Because of the atmosphere, the Briton's could not function as normal guardians. The threat of discovery was pervasive. As Mr. Yueling's endeavors expanded, Lee Briton took on a larger role in negotiating new routes, carriers, and vetting resources. Their lives were under a microscope. As such, Elijah's existence was confined to the homestead.

"Elizabeth came from a family of educators, so she easily transitioned between Elijah's caregiver and his tutor. She loved to read and write, a trait she passed on to my grandfather. Printed material was not easy to attain so on the rare occasions when they went to town, Elizabeth would purchase anything that contained pictures and articles to share with Elijah.

"She developed a close friendship with the mayor's wife who fancied herself an artisan. Mrs. Renault occasionally received magazines and newspapers from overseas vendors. When she discovered Elizabeth's interest, she was happy to pass them along.

"Elijah grew up with pictures of Native Americans, British soldiers, French royalty, and Spanish villas. As he matured, he longed to travel to these places, but more importantly, he wanted to capture the scenes he saw around him. The beauty of the swamps and the marsh lands, the birds, animals, and people he communed with daily. Grandfather created most of these while living with the Britons, but soon his heart yearned for more.

"He left the homestead in 1783. He was eighteen. He joined a group of slaves Lee was guiding to New York, and from there, he crossed the border into Canada. He worked as a fisherman for a few years. After several bouts with scurvy, he submitted an article to the local newspaper under the pseudonym of a local captain. The article gained such popularity among his seamen and the local fisheries that he continued. Eventually, the mayor got involved and the crews saw several improvements. Emboldened, Grandfather continued to write about other topics. He soon received a request from the editor to join the newspaper.

"The politics of slavery were visible; even in Canada. Though technically free, Grandfather realized he'd never see a dime if he came forth, so he negotiated that he'd continue to submit articles and the funds would be routed to Elizabeth and Lee in Charleston."

"In 1789, Grandfather moved in with a French woman named Isabella. They never married, but had three children and lived happily together until her death in 1800. When her family arrived for the funeral, they were surprised to discover that Grandfather was black and that there were three children.

"Discussions ensued, and it was decided that Isabella's family would take custody of the children and that Elijah would move to France to remain a presence until such time as they reached maturity."

"So there is a branch of the Briton family tree in France?"

"Yes. Every year we transport a portion of Grandfather's collection to the sister site in Roussillon where Isabella's family still resides."

"How long did Elijah reside in France?"

"He traveled and studied throughout the country until his oldest daughter married in 1813. He returned to Toronto with his second wife and son in 1815."

Ayreal walked over to a small desk and picked up a leather bound portfolio. She handed it to Joseph. "These are some of Elijah's early sketches."

Joseph's hands were shaking as he pulled the strings from the edges. He pulled out two chairs and motioned towards one while taking Ayreal's hand. She sat and watched him do the same.

Joseph placed the object on the table between them and opened the cover. The first was a laminated drawing of a man on a boat in the middle of a grove of weeping willows. He turned to the next and saw a scatter of birds in flight over a tiny outhouse. The third was of a group of men standing at the entrance to a tunnel, shovels and picks over their shoulders and in the background, a tiny little girl with a doll looking up at them as they descended into the darkness. Joseph felt a chill run over his shoulders.

"If you look closely, you can see the date and his initials embedded in the seams of the men's clothing. It was a game he and Elizabeth played. The majority of his works contain the same signature."

"How did you find these?"

"When Elijah returned to the homestead for the funeral, he found these and some of the others in the basement. Elizabeth had packed everything in a box Lee had made for her with Grandfather Elijah's name engraved on the front."

Joseph continued to flip through the pictures until he came to one near the end. It was of a group of boys, standing on the river bank. Joseph mentally counted each one, memorizing their shape and size. When his eyes moved to the three in the back, he noted the shirtless teen with the rope around his chest and his arm around each of the boys beside him. He searched the picture until he found the small notch in the charcoal penciled line, 1772. He was looking at a photo from Elijah's memory; his and Matthew's last moment with Adam.

Elijah had drawn the vision like the photos he'd seen in periodicals where the subjects stared into the lens, their eyes focused on the photographer, waiting for his command before the flash of light captured their thoughts and dreams for the world to critique. No one would know the story behind this picture. People could only imagine where each of these boys would reside in history. Their lives to most folks would be relegated to this framed image but Joseph knew the story, and now as he ran his finger across the outline of the tiny faces staring blankly at him from time's crucible, he felt Adam exhale.

"That was one of my father's favorites. He remembered when it hung in the window of Grandfather's house."

"I'd like a copy of it if I may."

"Certainly. I'll have Jersey prepare a copy and mail it to your office in New York."

"Thank you."

Joseph laid the photo down. He touched the three figures in the back one final time before closing the portfolio. When he looked up, Aryeal was watching him intently.

"You did not accept my invitation merely to hear Grandfather's story did you, Mr. Iglaysia?"

"No, ma'am."

Joseph reached into his backpack and pulled out a small package. He placed it on the table and removed the layers of fabric covering the object. He pushed the necklace over to Ayreal and waited for her reaction.

"I believe you have one of these in your possession as well."

Ayreal hesitated before picking up the necklace. She twirled the twine between her fingers and smiled. When she looked up at Joseph, she had tears in her eyes.

"My father gave me Grandfather's at my wedding. I passed it to my oldest son when he graduated from high school. His oldest son just turned thirteen. We've scheduled a dinner here for the occasion. My son will give it to him then."

Ayreal Montgomery reached across the table and took Joseph's hand in hers and squeezed it gently.

"Adam can finally rest with his brothers."

Joseph sat quietly. He was not surprised or even amazed that Ayreal knew the source of his quest. His experience with Taylor had taught him that the universe, though massive, was still intricately connected through the individuals within its grasp. He'd found the end to Adam's story and now it was time to finally write his own.